ADDENDUM TO
A PHOTO ALBUM

VLADISLAV OTROSHENKO

ADDENDUM TO A PHOTO ALBUM

A NOVEL

TRANSLATED FROM
THE RUSSIAN
BY LISA HAYDEN

DALKEY ARCHIVE PRESS
Champaign / London / Dublin

Originally published in Russian as Prilozhenie k fotoal'bomu
by Vremya, Moscow, 2007

Library of Congress Cataloging-in-Publication Data
Otroshenko, Vladislav, author.
[Prilozhenie k fotoal'bomu. English]
Addendum to a photo album / by Vladislav Otroshenko ;
translated from the Russian by Lisa Hayden.
pages cm
I. Hayden, Lisa C., translator. II. Title.
PG3484.2.T76P7513 2014
891.73'5--dc23
2014028693

The publication was effected under the auspices of the Mikhail
Prokhorov Foundation TRANSCRIPT Programme to Support
Translations of Russian Literature

Partially funded by the Illinois Arts Council, a state agency,
and by the National Endowment for the Arts, a federal agency.

www.dalkeyarchive.com

Printed on permanent/durable acid-free paper
Cover design and composition Mikhail Iliatov

TRANSLATOR'S INTRODUCTION

Writing is reputedly a lonely activity, but translating Vladislav Otroshenko's *Addendum to a Photo Album* felt like anything but a solitary pursuit, despite all the weeks and months I spent alone in my office with only the Internet and two junior cats. *Addendum* is so filled with characters—the majority of them a clan of peculiar Cossack "uncles" and their parents, wives, and in-laws—that "alone" wasn't an option as I unraveled sentences describing the family's photo sessions, unusual relationships, military service, and meandering home. That unraveling often required significant time: Otroshenko loves writing sentences as long as the Don River, sentences that give his writing a flow so important to his storytelling that I couldn't bear to interrupt them with full stops that would have felt like dams. Instead I used commas, dashes, and semicolons to reroute, reorder, and rearrange his words.

Humor and absurdity are important elements in Otroshenko's writing, too. The first time I spoke with him about the book, during a Skype call allegedly unrelated to the translation, I jokingly asked about a passage where insects are reputed to make honey freeze, or somehow solidify. The phrase about the honey had generated a lengthy conversation with two native speakers of Russian who'd heard me read an excerpt from the book at the American Literary Translators Association conference in October 2013. Nobody had a problem with the long sentences and the humor seemed to work, but the honey thing made no sense to them … or me, either, to be honest, though my intuition told me there was nothing wrong with my translation. Intuition is a powerful force in translation, though of course I'd consulted the all-knowing Google, where I'd hoped to learn about some obscure Russian superstition related to, perhaps, storing honey near insects that aren't bees. But I found nothing. And then Otroshenko told me he'd simply made up the insect-honey connection because it sounded absurd. I couldn't argue with that. And we laughed.

It's common knowledge that writers, particularly of fiction, make things up and expand on what's conventionally known as reality, but I should alert readers of this translation, as a sort of public service announcement, that Otroshenko has a particular skill for creating an atmosphere in which a slightly stretched reality feels strangely and, to my mind, almost perfectly plausible. Even so, when I ran across the glass (h)armonica in *Addendum*, I initially thought Otroshenko had invented this impossible-sounding instrument—I pictured something shaped like a typical metal harmonica but made of ridiculously thin glass—rather than Benjamin Franklin, who really, truly did create a freestanding instrument known as the glass armonica, a contraption with rotating glass disks. Franklin was apparently inspired by the sound of a wet finger on the rim of a wineglass. (I highly recommend asking Google for a link to a video of the glass armonica.) As a translator, it was particularly fun to watch how Otroshenko's quirky and imaginary inventions—super-sensitive honey, fantastical mustaches, a house that feels as big as the world—blend organically with inventions, such as the glass armonica, that truly do exist but seem at least as strange as fiction. It's no wonder I smiled whenever I sat down to work on *Addendum*.

The "truly does exist" category also applies to the novel's historical backdrop: the book takes place in the early twentieth century and contains references to World War I and various historical figures. Otroshenko's Mandrykins are Cossacks, and their patriarch, Malach, is a born warrior who sees war and killing as justified. When Otroshenko and I talked about Cossackdom, he quoted poet Velimir Khlebnikov, who once wrote that Russian literature barely notices Cossacks and also compared them to Japanese samurai. Otroshenko describes Cossacks as fighters with Turkic, Scandinavian, and Slavic roots, a cosmopolitan, separate, and fearless people who were always free, both internally and externally, people who served the Tsar mili-tarily but were never serfs under the gentry.

With Cossack warriors come Cossack uniforms, military structures, and ranks that don't always translate smoothly into English. Most items of clothing, such as the *papakha*, a hat, can, to some extent, be explained in the text, though hat fanciers might want to consult the Internet to see photos of *papakhas*, particularly since

Addendum contains two kinds, one of which, the "mountain *papakha*," is often fluffy and almost wig-like. Other terms, such as "host," used for army, may be more familiar. As for ranks, after consulting with both Otroshenko and Dalkey editor, West Camel, I italicized and glossed certain Cossack ranks that are somewhat familiar in English: a *yesaul*, for example, is a Cossack captain. I'm very grateful for West's edits to my manuscript later in the process, too, since they strengthen many sentences.

Two other categories of words created very specific questions. Most obsolete measures didn't seem to demand explanation, because of their context, though I couldn't resist adding a vodka-based equivalent for *shtof*, a term that can refer to either a unit of measure or a bottle, often four-sided, that contains a standard amount of liquid. And then there are words for extended family members: Russian has far more specific words for in-laws than does English, and I sometimes felt lost in a game of logic as I tried to figure out who was whom from whose perspective. I'm extremely fortunate to have my own host: friends and colleagues who endlessly offered to help me make sense of these and other questions.

Finally, every text contains words I think of as having broad horizons of opportunity, words that can be translated in many ways. I tortured Otroshenko with a slew of these broad words, asking open-ended, purposely naïve questions about how he saw and heard them so I could decide what English words or phrases felt like they would give optimal blends of meaning and sound to the translation. For example, I opted for "harpy" over "harridan" as a translation for *sterva*, because Otroshenko quoted the Russian with such gusto— "harridan" just didn't feel like it had enough power.

Literary translation isn't at all a lonely profession for me because I have so many friends and colleagues—frolleagues, really—willing to supplement my knowledge and the contents of all my paper and electronic dictionaries. I am grateful to all of them for helping me improve the text and avoid mistakes and blunders of various types. Lots of people ask about the translation process so I'm grateful for this opportunity to both thank those who collaborated with me, and offer a little more insight into how the book was translated. Any errors or infelicities in the translation are, of course, my responsibility.

Vladislav Otroshenko was extraordinarily helpful, answering my open-ended, purposely naïve questions about individual words and phrases with good humor and detail, and discussing Cossack history with me, too. Meeting Otroshenko twice in Moscow, before I began working on *Addendum*, was also helpful, because knowing a writer's voice and mannerisms helps me find a tone and voice for my translation. I think that's especially important with a voice that is—both in real life and on paper—as nuanced and playful as Otroshenko's.

Otroshenko did me another very good turn by sending me Anne-Marie Tatsis-Botton's French-language translation of *Addendum*. Though my Russian overshadowed my French decades ago and I can't fully appreciate its humor and vocabulary, her translation often offered ideas on word choice and helped me make decisions about difficult passages. Perhaps most importantly, I am a grateful borrower of her word "luminoscribe" as a translation for Otroshenko's *svetopisets*: though the Russian word, which Otroshenko uses at times for photographer, contains more wordplay than luminoscribe, luminoscribe far surpasses, both in meaning and elegance, any options I considered inventing, and I'm excited to extend its realm by including it in my English version of *Addendum*. I should add that *svetopisets* is not a common word. Its roots refer both to someone who "writes" with light and someone who describes the world, a nice combination. *Svetopisets* also rhymes with *letopisets*, a word for which the *Oxford Russian Dictionary* offers the translations "chronicler" and "annalist."

Liza Prudovskaya pored over an early draft of my translation, comparing it with the original, answering numerous questions about context and usage in Russian and English, and finding more odd mistakes than I'd care to count. Mary Lynch read a closer-to-final draft of *Addendum*, noting obscure words, some of which I subsequently glossed or changed, and alerting me to an ugly little bouquet of typos I'd missed on multiple readings. I'm also grateful for comments from translators who attended my reading at the 2013 ALTA conference, particularly Olga Bukhina, who read the opening pages of my early draft as we vainly attempted to come to terms with the frozen honey. My husband, Park, is a very patient translator's spouse: he ate lots of grilled cheese sandwiches and easy pasta dishes when I was working long hours, and answered numerous questions about the usage of historical and military words even, I admit, as we ate those hastily prepared meals. And therein, I suspect, lies the heart of whatever this alleged process of translation encompasses: a head that never stops considering and reconsidering the meanings and sounds of words.

Lisa Hayden, 2014

ADDENDUM TO
A PHOTO ALBUM

Dedicated to those dear and indelible figures who give me no peace even here, in the lost kingdom of Druk Yul, on the banks of the rapid-flowing Chinchu.

— The Storyteller, Kingdom of Bhutan, Thimphu, undated

PART I
AFRICA

After Uncle Semyon's side-whiskers burned up, he declared a period of mourning in the house, ordered all the mirrors be draped in black sateen, then donned a black suit with a satin collar that stank so much of mothballs, all the mosquitoes and flies in the house up and flew away.

Toward evening he sent identical telegrams to all his brothers:

DEPART IMMEDIATELY, SON. AN INFERNAL FIRE DEVOURED MY SIDE-WHISKERS. SEMYON MALA-CHOVICH.

He was not the eldest of the uncles, nor were his side-whiskers the most substantial—the eldest uncle, Porphiry Malachovich, had side-whiskers to his shoulders and was, himself, so vast that he had difficulty squeezing through certain doors—but for some reason Uncle Semyon had taken to calling all the uncles *son*, perhaps because he lived in and managed the house where they had been born, or perhaps because Annushka, who had birthed all the uncles into the world, loved him more than the others.

Uncle Semyon maintained that Annushka had kept his birth a secret from Malach, a brainless and decrepit idol who was certainly not his father—someone incapable of bringing anything into the world beyond the monster who was Uncle Porphiry, or the mediocrity who was Uncle Josya, whom Annushka, either from forgetfulness or from empathy for Josya's sickly frailness, stubbornly called "my little youngest one," investing a grain of condescending tenderness into those innocent words. Words that irritated Uncle Semyon no end. If Annushka so much as uttered them after mentioning poor Uncle Josya, Uncle Semyon would be stricken with something resembling a seizure: he would suddenly stop in the middle of the room and freeze in an agonized pose, as if a beam had been lowered onto his neck. He would stand for some time in one place, his eyes light blue, like January icicles, and furiously turning, until the indignation caught in his throat finally discovered his tongue, which cast it into unthinkable expressions.

"Oh, monstrous old woman!" Uncle Semyon would exclaim,

jerking his head up and shaking his splayed fingers in the air. "Oh, mellifluous harpy!" he would say after a short pause, seeking the most effective intonation for the grandiose tirade already waiting to break free from his chest, unimpeded by any of the hesitations and obstacles that his ever-vigilant actor's instinct had placed in its path. "Oh, deranged woman, how many times must I remind you who sprang—to the woe of the Universe—from your unbridled womb, when, and in what succession!"

It was impossible to ascertain what woe Uncle Semyon meant. Nobody doubted, however, that, of all the uncles in the world, it was certainly he whom the Universe had impatiently awaited as he languished in Annushka's womb like an inmate in a dungeon, installed there not by some whim of chance, like all the other uncles, but by the will of Providence itself; or that the Universe rejoiced when the mysterious gates of flesh finally swung open before Uncle Semyon at the appointed time; or that myriads of stars glistened with a joyous light in the endless expanse of the cosmos when Uncle Semyon's first cry filled Malach's residence. But Uncle Semyon never explained why the Universe was concerned with the other uncles, or how they had distressed it.

Many miracles and omens accompanied Uncle Semyon's birth. During the year he came into the world, a northern wall in Malach's vast house suddenly collapsed in the middle of the night, revealing a hitherto unknown room. This was a spacious, hexagonal hall gleaming with polished parquet and freshly whitewashed walls; a completely brand-new chandelier of gilded bronze and colored glass, untouched by dust and resembling an inverted crown, graced the ceiling. It was under this very chandelier that Uncle Semyon would later deliver all his monologues and wrathful speeches, addressing the thirteen chubby little angels Malach himself had sculpted on the ceiling: these curly-haired babies, with their short, little wings, performed a joyful dance around the chandelier, harmoniously holding hands and flying in a cheerful gust, forming an unbreakable circle that was a "symból of unity" between all thirteen uncles, as wise Uncle Seraphim explained to his countless in-laws, since he understood the mysterious meaning of his parent's pronouncements and actions better than the rest.

The little angels were Uncle Semyon's most devoted and patient listeners. Sometimes he called them stinking devils and shouted that he would smash the entire whoring pack of them with a hammer if they didn't stop smiling Malach's idiotic smile, which Malach had intentionally created on their faces so the scoundrels could always mock Uncle Semyon's speeches. But there were moments when Uncle Semyon was filled with tenderness for the little angels. He would point at them and say that a great day—The Day of Universal Awakening—would soon arrive. And then, Uncle Semyon would say, glancing at the little angels, his eyes filled with affectionate, sweet tears, and then these dear, tiny ones, these joyful babes, these purest offspring of the ether, will come to life, rouse themselves, and fly, spreading their little, snow-white wings, their bright faces gleaming, scattering around the world to proclaim everything they had heard from Uncle Semyon in that loathsome corner, where nobody had ever understood his fervent feelings, his noble ambitions, or his intentions and speeches about the greatness of Brotherly Love and the nonentities that were the uncles, who had only appeared in the world to fatten themselves at their apiaries, as did Uncle Porphiry, or wither away at a reeking gasoline station, as did Uncle Josya. No, Uncle Semyon shouted, shaken by his own eloquence, these walking testimonies to the repulsive, elderly lust of a half-dead madman who had dared lodge his despicable seed in a place specially prepared for just Uncle Semyon, would never be elevated to the heights of Love.

It was under that chandelier, too, that Uncle Semyon spake the horrid prophesy that cost him fractured collar and hip bones. It was due to sheer luck that he didn't die, for on that ill-fated day he had got it into his head to come home from the theater in the cardboard armor of some ancient knight or other. He walked around the house in it the entire evening, removing neither his false beard nor the large, bushy eyebrows that were glued to his forehead and protruded menacingly from under a wooden helmet thickly painted silver. That helmet saved Uncle Semyon when the chandelier came down on his head just after he'd announced to poor Annushka, who was fright-ened to death by his appearance, that she should stop everything and prepare wood for Malach's coffin.

"For that worthless stone idol's hour of demise," Uncle Semyon managed to say, "his hour of demise is at hand! ..."

In reality, by this time, The Immortal One was already overcome with infirmity. He had withered and shrunken in size to such a degree that it took some effort to seek him out in the small, dark storage room where he slept continuously, surrounded by rags and all manner of castoffs. Malach had settled into his storage room immediately after creating the final uncle; this being Izmail, an uncommonly lively and animated uncle. He was as round, sturdy, red-cheeked, and pudgy as a matryoshka doll. Everything about him was pudgy: his neck, his arms, his legs, and even the fingers strewn with little gray hairs on his puffy little palms. Uncle Izmail, like all the uncles on earth, came into the world with side-whiskers. In Malach's house, however, nobody attached any particular meaning to this fact. And it was only Uncle Porphyry—who had begun speaking more and more frequently about his own loneliness and about the ailments and closeness of old age, and who had even begun using a walking stick a few days before Izmail's birth—who showed any exceptional excitement. No sooner had Uncle Izmail been swept into the bright rooms of Malach's home by a life-giving wave, after wallowing for billions of centuries in a remote, pitch-black abyss, than did Uncle Porphyry, who'd been impatiently awaiting him all year, grab the newcomer in his arms, carefully inspect him, and shriek, for the whole house to hear, "Long live the tribe with congenital side-whiskers!"

Porphiry's own side-whiskers, which were densely sprinkled with silvery little sparks, had already thinned out in certain places, but they were still holding their pillar-like form and a lively resilience in their spreading ringlets, and looked especially grand that day. It was said that when Uncle Izmail smiled and, after catching sight of them, grasped his elder brother's side-whiskers—to the boy's delight, a bee had just flown out of them, turning somersaults for the baby's pure enjoyment—the elder uncle was so touched that it took him some time to compose himself. Porphiry hovered around Izmail all day, now trying to feed him from a honeycomb, now fondly watching him, then suddenly leaning over the cradle, rounding his fleshy cheeks, blushing hard from joyful zeal, and blowing with all his might into a mouth organ that emitted juicy sounds and gleamed brightly under his mustache. About five months later, according to the uncles' stories, Porphiry raced over in a quick, two-wheeled cart, hatless and tipsy at the crack of dawn, and took Izmail away to his own *stanitsa*, ostensibly to take him for a ride to that Cossack village, but in fact never returning him to Annushka. He reared him in the *stanitsa* according to his own understanding of things. Many in the house later claimed it was in fact Uncle Porphiry who had accustomed the baby first to honey, and then, little by little, to mead, making it his fault that the youngest uncle, despite all his cheerfulness and even a certain inquisitiveness, never displayed the slightest signs of a mature mind. Uncle Izmail lived to the depths of old age (never, however, looking old) at the apiary on Uncle Porphiry's estate and, never cognizant of anything but always filled with good spirits, battled for days on end with spiders, flies, butterflies, and numerous other inconceivable insects seemingly capable of *freezing the honey*.

There were also claims that the younger brother's feeblemindedness completely suited Uncle Porphiry, who, they say, bought him a small firearm and a felt cap with a feather, equipping him to guard his enterprise. But this was all a malicious invention: Uncle Porphiry did value abundance, but he was not so miserly as to impede the small thefts committed by peace-loving neighbors or the boy's dignified kin, who stopped by to inquire after his health and quietly carried something off—perhaps a rooster or a small cleaver. As for the daughters-in-law and sisters-in-law who paid him visits in whole hordes and stole on a large scale, well, they were not to be frightened by a small firearm (which they had probably invented themselves anyway), nor by Izmail's madness, nor, even more so, by a cap with a feather. They weren't even afraid of Uncle Porphiry himself. Toward the end of his long life, lived in toil and care, and carried out with rural piety, they assiduously cleaned him out, leaving him with but a dozen hives and an ottoman with a tattered bolster that stood in the house, orphaned among bare walls that gleamed with white spots: one pining for the mighty back of the sideboard, another for a colorful little rug.

It was remarkable that, though he was accustomed to living surrounded by solid objects and seeing life's fickleness through a haze
of reliable abundance, the loss of these former comforts and the obvious impoverishment of his enterprise did not distress Uncle Porphiry in the least. To the contrary: he met this ruin with a hussar's
bravado and an elated amazement. Sipping from a mug of mead, he
would go into the yard in a soiled *beshmet*, the same old quilted tunic
coat he'd worn long ago during his service in the Caucasus, happily
look around, knock his walking stick on the ground, and say, "So,
Izmail, they pilfered us! Ah, they pilfered us!"

And Uncle Izmail would joyously smile at his brother, though
he didn't understand what Porphiry meant. He would wink at him
in reply. He could show a bit of hussar bravado, too: he would suddenly slap himself on the thighs and sink to a squatting position with
a hoot, then tear off, hands on hips, all the way to the gate, then
further, onto the street and into the open.

Later, after Uncle Porphiry had passed away—not in the manner
he had dreamed of, not on feather pillows, but in dust, in the attic,
where he'd climbed to repair the chimney ("He was always bustling
about," said Annushka, "he couldn't sit around doing nothing")—
another opinion took shape regarding Uncle Izmail and the circumstances that, as it was evasively expressed in the household, served as
the reason for his *despondency*. His lively nature, reasoned the uncles,
and his unusual impressionability and anxious character demanded
special attention from his parent, whose wise heart, had it harbored
but a spark of parental tenderness, could have become a valuable source
of life-giving light within Izmail's dark soul. As it happened, said the
uncles, Malach lacked the tenderness. It had run dry even before the
birth of Izmail, who was, in their opinion, not the complete *idiot* certain of the uncles sometimes claimed, though it was, to be exact, always only one uncle, Uncle Semyon, who so enjoyed pronouncing
that scandalous word. Izmail's slumbering mind, immersed in the
chaos of erroneous concepts, might well have woken up completely,
the uncles convinced one another, might have developed over time,
perhaps even brilliantly, had Malach not abandoned the baby, had
he not disappeared without a trace for long years, settling, as it later

turned out, in the distant storage room. Or, the other uncles angrily said, had he deigned to at least show himself before the poor baby at the hour he came into the world! ...

The Immortal One wasn't even nearby at the time, however; nobody in the household knew where he was. On the day when he cast his ancient tackle into the deep sea of nonexistence for the last time and fished out Uncle Izmail, he was, according to Annushka's account, "as despondent as an old monkey." The Immortal One sat for a long time in her bedroom, huddling his entire small, light-brown body, which smelled of cold wax, on the leather divan with the tall bulging back, and touching his narrow chest with the long chin that hung nearly to his navel and was as hard as a cobblestone; he was looking at the portraits of the uncles that hung in three rows along the wall. The yellowed whites of his small, motionless eyes shone with dull amber twinkles from the deep sockets that were framed by rings of reddish hairs: these rings quivered unceasingly, sometimes narrowing, sometimes widening, and it seemed The Immortal One would begin to weep at any moment. But when he dressed and left the bedroom, a smile suddenly appeared on his face, first hardly noticeable, then more obvious. He smiled, glancing to one side, as if someone, some imp with a fluffy sprig of spring grass, were tickling him behind the ear. With that smile on his face, he set off somewhere, to the southern rooms, obviously, where he loved wandering in solitude. And then he got lost.

Annushka expressed the faint hope that The Immortal One would now, just maybe, finally lose his way in his own home, never again to find the road back to her bedroom: she was sick and tired of birthing and feeding the uncles. She said this in the presence of Uncle Semyon, and regretted it later, because Semyon had just then come home from a rehearsal and, still under the power of menacing and fervid rhetoric from some bilious military leader or other, became horribly agitated.

"Yes, yes," he said, rushing to reassure her, "the unfortunate woman may now breathe a sigh of relief, for Malach's time of generating nations from his loins has come to an end!"

To this he added some other dark incantations that were

incomprehensible to Annushka. He spoke at length, and with inspiration, about some unscrupulous god devouring his own babies, about a mad dragon doomed to swallow its own tail eternally, about a terrible monster tormenting a defenseless female place with its bloody jaws. Then he finished his tirade with a frightening dance under the chandelier and wild cries of "Ouroboros, Ouroboros! Vanish! Vanish!"

They didn't see Malach in the house for about forty years. Nobody even reminisced about him. And it was only Uncle Semyon who sometimes squeamishly breathed the air through, as he himself expressed it, his "sensitive actor's nose," and then announced that something reeked in the house.

"Ye gods!" he would say, gesturing with a handkerchief, "Malach took refuge in some corner and perished like a ferret!"

It goes without saying that Annushka could not bear to listen to speeches of this nature. Taking care to avoid using any of those insensitive words that directly name certain phenomena and objects any living soul would ÿnd distasteful, she emphatically assured Semyon that "there are no such odors" in the house. But Uncle Semyon was not to be paciÿed. He intimidated Annushka with orderlies. Holy mothers! He threatened her, saying he would call for them right now if she did not insist that all the uncles gather at once and seek out their parent's reeking remains. Annushka didn't know precisely who these orderlies were, but, nevertheless, she felt in her soul that their appearance in the house would be an "unheard-of disgrace"—something she could not allow. Be that as it may, she said—implying in her "be that as it may" the deplorable state of the human body Uncle Semyon had described in so harsh and inharmonious a way—she would not allow a proper home to be exposed as a laughing stock: she imagined the orderlies as either cemetery functionaries with unthinkable responsibilities and inclinations, or (and here it was di₍cult to understand her) a certain breed of bold and unruly gravediggers, hailing from the ranks of lapsed doctors, and brimming with monstrous artistry, to boot. In short, she essentially imagined this: Uncle Semyon would bring home some odious jesters from a country churchyard, and they would make horrendous faces and shamelessly ransack the house, pretending to search for a deceased person or some other foulness. No, repeated Annushka, she would never allow that. And if it appeared to Uncle Semyon that *something of that sort had happened*, she said, offended, then it was not because it actually had, but rather because Uncle Semyon had always regarded Malach with disrespect; but no matter what sort of parent Malach was, he was, after all, a parent to all the uncles, Uncle Semyon among them … Cross my heart, merciful apostles! And that is what she said to him: "Malach is your parent, Syomushka," and it was a great miracle that her tongue didn't dry up then and there, and that lightning didn't strike Malach's house, killing the unfortunate woman on the spot. In any case, Uncle Semyon expected something horrible to happen and stood for a moment, stooped and squinting; only later did he begin grasping himself—first his chest, then his head—and performing, in the usual order, the specific motions that always preceded his monologues under the chandelier.

This was, however, one of the rare situations when Uncle Semyon burst into speech not under the chandelier, but in Annushka's bedroom, where there were, so to speak, visual aids: photographic portraits of the uncles.

"The-ere!" he rasped, choking and shaking as if feverish. "All these … good-for-nothing hogs! These are Malach's true products!"

And just then his hand, as it stretched toward the portraits and nervously waved in the air, unexpectedly froze; he hid his other hand behind his back, took three paces forward (one might have thought the uncle had suddenly taken it into his head to rehearse the role of an impertinent duelist), and said with victorious, vindictive ardor, "Oh, God! All with the same face!"

And he was, of course, correct. The physiognomies of the uncles that looked out from the portraits, despite all their unquestionable variations, expressed primarily in the length and bushiness of their sidewhiskers and the absence or presence of mustaches—Uncle Nestor, for example, was content with a firm chainmail of "senatorial" sidewhiskers and had never worn a mustache, but then Uncle Pavel, Annushka's fourth son, had a mustache that positively ran amok on his face, "like King Victor Emmanuel," he would say, not without pride, laughing at Uncle Seraphim, whose elegant chevalier mustache was thin, thinner than a dragonfly's tail, and seemed to Uncle Pavel to be just about the most comical thing on earth—presented a picture of harmonious uniformity. They were all identically broad, with identically bulky chins, and identically merged eyebrows. Even Uncle Izmail's small, fat mug, which had appeared on the wall later than the rest, might well be taken as a reduced copy of the hefty physiognomy of the eldest uncle, along which ants openly strolled around as if they owned it, peering into the photograph's dusty cracks.

As for Uncle Josya, his portrait, which hung in the second row, between portraits of Uncle Nikita and Uncle Mokei (both wearing the uniforms of vakhmistrs—cavalry sergeant majors—both cheerily smiling at something), was the object of a separate and more detailed conversation. As it happened, through some vexing twist of fate, Uncle Josya did not resemble a hog at all, and so before he—he who was looking with either grateful curiosity or, on the contrary, with tremendous disgust at a little, decorated flower pot that a clever photographer had placed in front of him—could be attributed to the ranks of "Malach's true products," it had to be explained to poor Annushka that Uncle Josya, whom she treated with excessive tenderness, was not an exception to the rule at all, but rather a special variety of mediocrity.

It was with this in mind that Uncle Semyon took Uncle Josya's portrait down from the wall and ran to the hexagonal hall, most likely a more apt place for him to expound on "the question of Uncle Josya," since in this huge hall—which loudly sighed, ahhed, and, so it seemed, lightly quivered (the acoustics were that effective)—Uncle Semyon's voice sounded far more ceremonial and convincing than in the other rooms, even the most echoingly deserted and immense, rooms like those that Uncle Pavel had told about with horror after once being in the south of Malach's house, where he saw such terribly tragic, open spaces enveloped in lifelessness, and such a vicious cobweb, in which there hung lizards and, apparently, even chairs, that this chipper, convivial fellow returned with a gray side-whisker.

Uncle Semyon spoke at length in the hexagonal room, not pausing for even one instant. The walls, which concealed a resonant, staccato echo, and were hung with mirrors into which he gazed from time to time, noting the dramatic merits of a gesture he'd used or a pose he'd chosen, inspired him and imparted confidence. Uncle Semyon thought the hexagonal room had a salutary effect on Annushka, too, that she listened to him mindfully here, not as carelessly or absent-mindedly as elsewhere. He also thought it was only in that living, wonderful, and wonder-working hall that her small, idle little mind, befogged by false feelings for Uncle Josya, could illuminate with the light of Truth. But this was already a delusion, and a "fundamental" delusion at that, as Uncle Seraphim might have noted, had he suddenly been presented with the opportunity to deliberate on the reasons and consequences of all the delusions on earth. He would have deliberated unhurriedly, would have thoughtfully tugged at his thin little mustache during lengthy pauses (a gesture that brought Uncle Pavel to boisterous fits of merriment) and, finally, pointed out that excessive anxiety... hmm ... hmm ... deprives any person of insight, Uncle Semyon among them, since his excessive anxiety prevented him from noticing that Annushka was completely indifferent to where she listened to his explanations. She couldn't understand them in either the bedroom or the hexagonal room, to which she obediently relocated, following the orator: she generally had difficulty understanding the intricate language in which Syomushka expressed his feelings and thoughts during his moments of "scandalous temper."

Forgetting even to think about either Malach or the horrifying picture of the invasion of the orderlies that her ill-informed imagination so vividly painted, Annushka would sit submissively in a chair in the corner, sink into a sweet drowsiness, and try to grasp, with fading ear, which of the uncles Uncle Semyon referred to most frequently in his monologue. And if the unbroken flow of inconceivable and unfulfillable threats, monstrous oaths, prophesies, and incantations spewing forth from Uncle Semyon's breast, together with groans, sighs, and howls, enabled her to finally manage to recognize a distinctive little sliver (meaning Uncle Josya's name), rising up, over and over, to the surface of the dark, irrepressible rapids, she would open her eyes and say, as affectionately as possible, "Syomushka, why are you scolding Josya? He's so pitiful ..."

"P-p-p-pitiful?!" Uncle Semyon would yell. And then, brandishing the portrait, he would stomp and jump, circling under the chandelier as if a tarantula had stung him. "Pitiful!" he would repeat in a frenzied whisper, leaning forward, slowly closing in on Annushka, and ferociously moving his cheekbones, where his marvelous side-whiskers swayed, resembling tight, compact clusters of black grapes and emitting a fiery blueness. "I'll devour your despicable Josya!!!" he would hiss through his teeth, and then quieten down, waiting to hear what Annushka would say to that.

Annushka would fidget in the tall chair, animatedly swinging her little feet, wizened from endless bustling around the house, and silently looking at Uncle Semyon, hoping his performance was nearing its end. But then, as was wont to happen, Uncle Semyon would unexpectedly remember an intense epithet from a little play he'd read the day before, or a majestic comparison would suddenly come to mind, something that promised to become the beginning of a new "Regarding Uncle Josya's Innumerable Nasty Tricks" monologue, and he would again return to the place under the chandelier.

"Liiisten, aaangels," he would say in a singsong voice. "No, you just listen," he would insist, as if the angels had not agreed to listen. "Joseph Malachovich, fifth son of this woman, is piiiitiful! ... But he is a Judas! A Judas! He sold everything that was sacred in this unfortunate house!"

What could poor Uncle Josya—small, thin, bug-eyed, and resembling a surprised turkey poult—have sold? He never sold anything in his whole life other than fuel at his gas station, The Vulcan Well, which was untidy to an extreme and dangerously accessible to gawkers with burning cigarettes: it stood at the central gates of the Carriage Market, filling the air with suffocating fumes. But Uncle Semyon's view of things was not so superficial that he saw Uncle Josya as an inoffensive gasoline salesman. No: Uncle Josya had sold no more and no less than Uncle Semyon himself. And if Annushka's memory had failed her to the point that she had even forgotten who Uncle Semyon's father was, well, it stood to reason that it wasn't at all surprising that she didn't remember something else: she didn't remember that it was Uncle Josya himself who'd told Malach the sacred secret of Uncle Semyon's birth.

"Yes, yes! Your wonderful! … your meek! … and your most supremely despicable Josya!"

Of course Uncle Semyon did not permit the thought that the secret could have been given away by any of the uncles, particularly that Uncle Semyon himself could have given it away by claiming, despite Annushka's reprimands and timid objections and even occasional desperate protests, at every convenient opportunity—and especially in the presence of The Immortal One until, that is, he withdrew to his little storage room and, then again later, when he was found there, by chance, among battle paintings, worn basins, and vanished divans all heaped together in a pile—that his, Semyon's, father was apparently a Greek who was passing through, an incomparable artiste, a fabulously rich man, the owner of three circuses in China, and a sorcerer and seer besides. And of course, a handsome man, too, the likes of which the world had yet to see, just like Uncle Semyon, the ingenious Greek's secret son.

Malach was fighting in the First World War when Annushka and the Greek took it into their heads to create Uncle Semyon. Annushka, however, was not, initially, resolved to do it. She agonized fruitlessly for some time, her heart and soul burning with "the tempestuous flame of passion," and she even nearly lost her mind because of her infinitely tender feelings toward the Greek, with whom she furtively met, either under the canopy of the hundred-year-old chestnut trees in Large Hetman Garden, where his circus tent stood in the wind, covered in dragons and stars, or in the abandoned little square near the Cossack Host's clerical offices, where the small window of the *sotnik* on duty shone for them until dawn. "May it be blessed for the ages!" Uncle Semyon would say. "And may all the *sotniks*, all those Cossack lieutenants who were on duty at the clerical office, arrive in heaven!" Uncle Pavel would snidely add. He, as it happens, once swore, on the Holy Mother, that it was he who was on duty at the clerical office on those spring nights, and that he remembered extremely well both the ardent Greek under the linden trees (he saw him through the window) and Annushka in a colorful little shawl, arriving for their midnight trysts. It stands to reason that Annushka very much wanted to retain a memento of her mad love, something "live and trembling"—something akin to Uncle Semyon—but she feared Malach would not forgive her this weakness and that upon his return from the war he would certainly chop her in half with the devilishly sharp saber conferred on him for military valor by Russia's last emperor.

As it happened, however—on a fortunate day for Uncle Semyon—a certain injured warrior appeared in the house, all of a sudden, like an angel from the heavens. He was on one leg, all in bloody bandages, and wearing the uniform of a *yesaul*: a captain of the Cossack regiment's Imperial Guard. Pacing around the rooms on crutches and spitting saliva yellowed with tobacco smoke onto the parquet floors, his angry, hoarse voice told Annushka the story of Malach's horrible death. Oh, this was a monstrous story! He and Malach had been friends, after all, and it was difficult, very difficult, to tell the story. But the wounded warrior would tell it. There was an attack! There was shooting all around! And everyone being hacked! And everything was completely blown to hell. He and Malach ran, side by side, into the enemy's trenches. They shouted "Hurrah!"—and Malach ran like a brave fellow, shouting louder than them all and brandishing his saber like an enraged demon, and shot with good aim at everyone ... But then he fell behind a little and ran back a tiny bit, as the injured warrior ran ahead. And when the injured warrior turned his head back to look for Malach, he saw that his devoted friend was running, headless, his head having been chopped off long before. But Malach ran and ran, like a brave fellow. Heroically running all the way to the very trenches. With some effort, the injured warrior found Malach's head after the battle: it was lying quietly in the tall weeds, its mouth wide open, because of course Malach had been yelling "Hurrah!" the whole time ... And who chopped off his head? Oh, who can really know?! When they're shooting and chopping off heads every which way, all hell breaking loose!

Annushka didn't believe the warrior. She said something bitter and offensive to him; she said Malach had never run, that he'd always fought on a horse. But the injured warrior didn't utter a single word in response. He silently heard out Annushka's objections then untied the sack on his back, pulled out Malach's head, carefully placed it on the table, and left, tapping his crutches.

The Greek rushed over to see Annushka that same day. He was irresistible, her charming tormentor, her beloved wizard. He stood before her that day in his full grandeur. Uncle Semyon said that his unforgettable parent pulled up at Malach's home on one hundred and twenty circus horses harnessed in tandem to a golden chariot. Oh my, my, ye demons of Hell, it was so beautiful! He ran up the tall stairs to the front doors, opened both sides and entered, dressed in a white tailcoat and dark-blue turban decorated with a diamond feather. Light-blue streams of fire poured from his ears and hundreds of marvelous pearls rotated in his mustache like tiny planets: they illuminated his entire face with a barely perceptible radiance, delicately sparkling, scattering a pearlescent sheen and, upon the wizard's slightest movement, flashing brightly with little multicolored lights that instantly arranged themselves in peculiar constellations. Annushka was dumbfounded with amazement at seeing her handsome man: she wanted to tell him everything that had happened to Malach, but wasn't able to utter two words before he waved his hands, telling her in gestures that he already knew everything. As proof, he took his own head and lifted it, completely separating it from his body then lightly shaking it—can you imagine?—shaking it as if it were a jewelry box. And she suddenly opened her mouth wide and began shouting an extended "Hurraaaaah!" in Malach's own voice.

And then he approached Annushka, leaned toward her, and quietly said, "The *yesaul* was completely correct, precious Annushka … Your Malach will not return from the war."

He pronounced those sorrowful words with such loving agitation and such refined tenderness that Annushka swooned, right then and there. The Greek gathered her up in his arms and carried her off to the bedroom. And they chirped until midnight as if they were heavenly little birds; they showered each other with passionate vows and with quiet kisses. And at midnight, when the stars glittered over the city like crystals, they finally flowed together in embraces and, with the full agreement of their astonished hearts, conceived the best uncle in the world!

But Annushka was in for a surprise when another *yesaul* appeared eight months later. This one was in full dress uniform, with all his arms and legs, wearing snow-white gloves and a hat with a plume. He spoke with Annushka briefly, and also angrily, like the other Cossack captain who had preceded him. Glancing out the window with displeasure, he told her that her Malach was alive and would be returning from the war any day. As for that head, the one the injured warrior had brought to her, the captain concluded it was most likely not Malach's but someone else's ... or should I say another's? Or, well, how should I say it, damn them all, those heads! In devilish quantities. Just devilish! Lying around in frightful heaps in fields and in trenches. And no way in hell to sort out whose was whose! There were all kinds of heads, all kinds. There were heads that looked like his, the captain's, and like Malach's head, too, and even like the head of the Tsar himself! Because this was war! "War!" shouted the *yesaul* in a fit of ire.

And with that, he left.

The Greek did not even begin to wait for Malach's return. He packed up his sideshow booths, loaded the tents on a wagon, sat the Chinese dancers in charabancs, and departed for Africa in a hurry.

He came to say goodbye to Annushka on the eve of his departure. The scene was sorrowful but also filled with deep meaning. He sat, bent over, at the head of her bed, in a traveling coat with a small *sac voyage* on his knees, and despairingly whispered something in Greek as he wiped streams of hot tears from her cheeks with a handkerchief. These were words of prophecy. And if Annushka had understood Greek, then Uncle Semyon wouldn't have to drum into her head now what the Greek told her on that memorable night. And here is what he said: He said that Malach had escaped from Austrian captivity about a week ago, that he had mustered bandits, deserters, cripples, and harlots in the woods, shaved them all bare, sat them on horses, and, with this mongrel army, was posing as the Bhutan king and fighting his way home along the southwestern front. In about ten days, said the Greek, Malach would reach the Province of the Don Cossack Host and would make camp on the steppe near the western walls of his house. Then only one march would remain for him: to the front doors. But in the morning, as soon as all his gang put out their camp fires and mounted their horses, darkness will fall on the Sarmatian steppes, and a blizzard will blow up on the Don. And what a storm it will be, God help us! Kurgan stelae will be ripped from burial mounds and fly across the sky like wood shavings, turning head over heels in flashing whirlwinds. And Malach will also be lifted to the sky, and not only to the sky, precious Annushka: your Malach will fly away into a starry abyss! And he will drift for a long time, ferociously waving his saber in the mute expanses of the Universe. He will howl, horrifying the whole cosmos, and bug his eyes into the emptiness until they turn to glass from hunger and melancholy! And then, said the Greek, satanic winds will cast Malach somewhere far away, to the East, beyond the Khvalyn Sea and further, beyond the Karakums and even to the Himalayas! And before he arrives back from there, strewing damnation on the earth under the soles of his shoes, before he arrives at the walls of his residence, hungry and bitten by dogs and snakes, Annushka will give birth, painlessly and without throes, to the son of their midnight love, here, in this bedroom … Like all her sons, he will come into the world with side-whiskers. But these will be special side-whiskers, side-whiskers of regal beauty, though the Greek did not say a word about their unexpected burning resulting from Uncle Semyon's decision, out of boredom, to repair an old primus stove. They will protect her son from misfortunes and fate's blows, like sacred talismans. Many of the Greek's abilities, many of his worldly and otherworldly talents, will be passed down to the son. But may he use them with circumspection. May he keep them until the proper time. For these talents will not be granted him so he can follow in the steps of his parent, to squander them for the amusement of madmen in the circus booths and tents of this mournful planet. No, Providence had destined more for him than for the Greek! He will teach people to love one another. Because he and only he will know the words with which to expound to all people that there is nothing in the world more beautiful than Brotherly Love. There will not be so very many of these great words, with which the meaning of the Universe is revealed: perhaps three, or maybe four, excluding prepositions and interjections. He will pronounce them somewhere here, in the northern part of Malach's house, not far from Annushka's bedroom. And this will happen, all of a sudden, on some gray, unprepossessing day, which will later be called The Day of Universal Awakening. The Greek would purposely refrain from speaking now about when this joyous day would arrive, and his son would give no indication on the day. No, no, let his brothers—everyone from Porphiry to Izmail (the Greek already knew then that Annushka's last would be Uncle Izmail)—thirstily heed his speeches. Because—who could know!—three or four great words might fall from his lips at any time. And then ... Oh! Then what woe! Woe to those who did not notice them! And damnation to those who did not hear them!

That is what the Greek said in Greek.

And in Russian he told Annushka to name the secret fruit of their tender love Uncle Semyon and to give him to an orphanage before Malach's arrival. The Greek had already agreed with the shelter about everything. And paid lots of gold Russian money to everyone there who needed to be paid! ... In short, let him live a month or two at the orphanage. Then Annushka's womanly heart would tell her how to wrap that old dimwit Malach around her finger when he returns!

And with that, they parted. The Greek pressed his lips to Annushka's shoulder, imprinting it with a final kiss, then exited into the nocturnal expanse. The horses began neighing, the heads of the Chinese dancers sleepily rocked. The charabancs set off for Africa.

Certain pieces of news about the Greek's life reached Annushka after his departure. It became known that the Greek did not soon find himself in Africa. Losses and misadventures plagued him during his journey. Cossacks took nearly all his circus horses at the harsh Caucasian front, German deserters took his elephant in Iran, someone's vicious artillery bombarded his caravan with shrapnel in Mesopotamia, someone adroitly and underhandedly slaughtered his acrobats in Syria, and he himself was nearly hacked to death by a Turkish cavalryman in Egypt. He somehow got to the equator with Belgian troops, but calamities awaited him there, too. His Chinese dancers were stolen in the Congo where, incidentally, his shows were the greatest of triumphs. He contracted a fever in Uganda. And a short time later the Algerian magician who had latched onto him as far back as the Caucasus burned his circus ...

He returned to Europe with only his small *sac voyage*. For three years he wandered various countries, as destitute as God and without a kopeck in his pocket, until he entered into service as a soldier in the fabulously small army of the Most Serene Republic of San Marino.

The Greek served in the army like a brave fellow. He strode in parades better than anyone else and had an excellent bearing. The Captains Regent took notice of his fastidious service and of his valor and courage—"for glinting heart and proud gait," as stated in the order—and appointed the Greek head drum major of San Marino's army. Oh, Holy Virgin! reminisced the San Marino officers later, what inspiration and what delightful virtuosity!—how he rotated and tossed that flying, glistening baton into the air! And how the army and residents of San Marino rejoiced when the Greek, impassioned and stern, all dressed in flames of golden thread, festively strode in parades ahead of the drummers and flutists!

Uncle Semyon said the drum major position brought the Greek, who served selflessly, the bit of capital that would have been sufficient to open, for example, a wine factory or small theater. But the Greek was in no hurry to part with his tiny army; only this sort of army, he said, with its courage amid the splendor of its parades, and valor in the grace of its stride, would behold the carefree dawn of the Day of Universal Awakening. "You, soldiers of my soul! And you, officers of the heart," the Greek said, roused, "you will enter the golden doors on the final day, in parade march, and illuminated by the glisten of unfading bugles! Yes, soldiers, it will be the final day, and it will be the first and eternal day, because it will be a singular, bright day for an entire universe awakened for love! And that is why I am teaching you today. No, I am ordering you, my dear ones. Hear out my order. Unite valor with love and may that which arises from them be your weapon! Fuse tenderness with bravery in your hearts: that gleaming fusion will be the kernel of your fury, the lead in your glimmering bullets! May your love be higher than bravery, your valor higher than love. But may valor never be higher than all-consuming tenderness. For tenderness will be the sun and the stars, and the sky and the light, and the essence of the light of the Day of Universal Awakening. You will enter that day, soldiers! But I will not go—He, the Founder of the Universe, will be your drum major! He will head up the parade procession and lead you, the brave ones, to the square where His white-winged angels will greet you."

That is what the Greek taught the San Marino army.

After serving a while longer and receiving a chivalry decoration for his civilian and military contributions—Uncle Semyon could no longer say what exact degree it was—the Greek retired after all: he had dreamt of a contemplative solitude, something he'd sorely lacked his entire life. In keeping with his dream, the Captains Regent ordered that a small home with carved pilasters and a little window facing south be built for the Greek in a quiet myrtle grove on the slope of Mount Titano. The retired drum major lived in the house in complete seclusion—two soldiers of the Guardia Nobile protected his tranquility—and wrote a book of prophesies of the Day of Universal Awakening. Then he left the manuscript of the book on his desk and disappeared. And neither the guardsmen nor the Captains Regent of the Most Serene Republic of San Marino knew anything further of his fate. His little house, as one San Marino patrician later told Annushka, was quickly transferred to the army's possession. San Marino officers who were friends of the Greek decided right then and there to open a museum in the house; they wanted to call it the Museum of Valor and Love. Exhibits were gathered: drums, horns, flutes, and certain various posters, one bought in China and two from the Sultan of Brunei, where the Greek had toured in the long-bygone years before he'd met Annushka. In the most visible place, directly above the desk, where the book of the Greek's prophesies lay under a bell jar, they hung the drum major uniform and the baton with which the Greek had achieved glory and widespread respect in the Most Serene Republic.

Among the various exhibits that the San Marino officers had carefully collected and placed in the Greek's house was a photograph of Annushka that had been found in his small *sac voyage*, the very same bag he took to Africa, where it was scratched up by dense vegetation. The photograph was taken in July 1914. Annushka was holding down her flat hat and standing on the sidewalk of Platovsky Avenue, near the Host's guardhouse building. A dull, dusty ray of midday sun was shining diagonally across the building: a sentry's leg hung in the air, and a quick-tempered little dog, who was eagerly flinging itself at the leg, just happened to fall into that drowsy ray, too, where they were conspicuous with the pointless and troublesome distinctness that images of secondary importance acquire in treasured photographs. Another of these secondary images was the broad back of someone's head in a white, civilian peaked cap: the head was disappearing (but had not disappeared) into the high, dark doorways of the guardhouse where Annushka had gone almost daily that summer to visit Uncle Nikita, who was there under arrest for talking back to an under-officer during the Don Cavalry's camp exercises. This under-officer was very important, from the Hetman Regiment's Imperial Guard; he was even a recipient of the Order of Saint Stanislav. And though Uncle Nikita also held a third-degree Stanislav, with gold swords and a ribbon, bestowed on him for reckless bravery in the Russo-Japanese War, it didn't save him from arrest: he'd answered the under-officer of the Imperial Guard far too sharply when the other, after noticing a blunder that Uncle Nikita allowed during the formation of the cavalry rearguard, took it upon himself to instruct him, in lengthy and endlessly courteous terms, about how one should properly command cavalrymen.

"I do hope you understand everything?" said the under-officer, concerned because Uncle Nikita was absentmindedly looking away.

"The worm!" said Uncle Nikita, loudly and distinctly, as if he'd regained consciousness. He then headed off to his trotter, but was immediately taken under guard, by order of a colonel who happened to be nearby ...

Of course, the San Marino officers knew nothing of this, just as they knew nothing of how Roman Khodetsky, a reporter from *The Don Cavalry Leaflet*, had photographed Annushka with a Lasker and Shtuhlman camera near the guardhouse—it was to Khodetsky that the Greek owed his acquaintance with "the *yesaul's* charming wife" ("The *yesaul's* charming wife," was written in Russian, in the Greek's hand, on a thick, lilac passe-partout with the embossed seal of the Province of the Don Cossack Host). Khodetsky placed the photograph on the fourth page of *The Leaflet* and composed a politely reproachful caption to accompany it:

The mother of Cavalry Sergeant Major Nikita Malachovich Mandrykin, who caused an uproar during cavalry exercises, came to visit her son at the guardhouse, where he is currently under arrest, and from which he will be set free only at the behest of the Host's hetman-in-charge, after he has become personally acquainted with all the circumstances of this incident. We already wrote in detail about it last week. We will simply remind the reader that the cavalry sergeant major in question displayed an unheard-of disrespect for his superior officers. This case is particularly dolorous because it casts a shadow on the cavalry sergeant major's most esteemed parent, Malach Grigorevich, who was recently promoted to the rank of yesaul of the Imperial Guard of the Cossack Regiment of His Majesty the Emperor, as well as the prisoner's brothers: Mokei Malachovich, also a cavalry sergeant major, and sotnik Pavel Malachovich. The Host's leadership speaks of both men in the very best of terms. As far as the mother of the arrested man is concerned, as she told us, she regards her son's behavior with condemnation, further remarking that Nikita Malachovich sincerely regrets the thoughtlessness of his actions.

The very next day, the Greek hurried to Komitetskaya Street, to the editorial offices of *The Leaflet*. He paid the reporter three entire gold imperials for the photograph! And the same amount for a promise that Annushka be brought to an evening circus performance.

She came two weeks later, accompanied by Khodetsky and Uncle Pavel, who was, for some reason, wrapped in a black cloak and armed with a revolver: Uncle Pavel himself didn't explain why, limiting himself to confirming, and fairly willingly so, Uncle Semyon's account. "Yes, yes," he said, taking on a dignified air, "that's how it all was, son. There was a revolver and a black cloak, and a broadsword beneath the cloak."

As soon as the audience had settled in their seats at the circus, the ringmaster solemnly came out in a short red jacket and announced the following, word for word, "Ladies and Gentlemen! Most esteemed public! We are giving today's performance in honor of one personage in attendance! In order not to embarrass her, we will use only her delicate, given name, Annushka … Annushka, the flame of love is burning in a heart that is, as yet, unknown to you. Henceforth it will forever be yours! Do watch, precious one: Chinese dancers will prance for you. Abyssinian acrobats will tumble for you. And we will perform marvelous magic tricks for you, incomparable Annushka! Oh, Annushka!"

Uncle Semyon said that a terribly rapturous din broke out in the circus. Uncle Pavel leapt up and shot into the air with his revolver. Other officers shot, too. And some visiting cavalry captain of Her Majesty's *Uhlan* Regiment ran onto the ring, grasped his head and yelled, "Oh, what love! What love, gentlemen!"

But the San Marino officers didn't know that, either.

The only thing they could have guessed—if, of course, the date written in pencil on the back of the photograph hadn't rubbed off, and if they had somehow miraculously learned that Annushka's son was sitting in the guardhouse—was that Uncle Nikita was released very soon without any investigation whatsoever, because of the start of the war, that great struggle between peoples. A struggle so great and so merciless that even the small, Most Serene Republic of San Marino, which wished for nothing but love and tranquility, could not stand aside: shaken by its scale and the fury of the battles that broke out, San Marino sent fifteen warriors and an aeroplane to assist the powerful and uneasy states of the Entente.

To be frank, however, the San Marino officers, abounding as they were in discretion, made not the slightest effort to ascertain the concealed and unprinted something that washed wordlessly—as dark lake waters wash a sandy little island—over an ancient photograph that had dulled quite considerably, either from time or the harmful vapors of equatorial swamps. In the explanatory caption that accompanied the photograph, the San Marino officers stated only that which they knew for certain, adding nothing of their own, nothing complicated or untrue. They simply wrote, "L'amica del greco,"[1] and

---

1 "The Greek's beloved" (Ital.)

that was enough for the museum in the tiny house on the slope of Mount Titano, which they wanted to call the Museum of Valor and Love, and which, to the great chagrin of Uncle Semyon and all the residents of San Marino, was never opened because lightning—may it be cursed!—from the capricious Apennine skies struck the Greek's little house and burned it down instantly before the astounded warriors' eyes. And it would have been one thing had it been only the little house, but the book of prophecies burned, too.

They were able to find only one burnt scrap of paper amidst the ashes and dust of the lamentably charred ruins. And it bore a striking resemblance to Africa! Each time he mentioned this enigmatic fact, Uncle Semyon mournfully bent his handsome head to his shoulder and said he personally saw a certain tragic meaning in the brutal flame devouring the great manuscript in its madness, choking on an unfortunate scrap of paper whose edges reflected with surprising precision, as if painstakingly traced by the hand of a conscientious cartographer, all the projections and bends of the resplendent continent so boundlessly dear to him and so boundlessly distant from our Sarmatian steppes, the continent where Uncle Semyon's unforgettable parent had feverishly wandered in the aforementioned years, carelessly squandering talents, money, and the crystalline days of his impassioned youth!

One line, written in the Greek's hand, was preserved on the Africa-shaped piece of paper. It stretched from north to south—sometimes disappearing in scorched holes—from the Libyan desert through the Ennedi Plateau, across the Ubangi and Congo Rivers, then following the current of the Zambezi, flowing to Drakensberg, then taking a sharp turn to the west and breaking off at the Cape of Good Hope.

These words were in that line:

" . . . And there will be love for you . . . my golden ones . . . open your eyes and rejoice . . ."

PART II
SYMBOLS

Semyon was born before Malach's return, as the Greek had predicted. And his birth was just as grand and mysterious as his conception.

Miraculously, the windy April night when Annushka's contractions began was the same night Uncle Pavel suddenly turned up, as if he'd been resurrected, having flown over Persia in reconnaissance aeroplanes all winter and—or so they informed Annushka—being taken prisoner by the Turks near Kermanshah along with an English aeronautical ace.

He pulled up at the house at three o'clock in the morning as if nothing had happened, as if he'd just gotten off a night shift: he was driving the clerical office's white Dux with its stitched burgundy seats, which he drove like a daredevil, lighting cigarettes along the way, and taking pleasure in frightening equestrians and pedestrians with the booming klaxon horn. Pavel looked vivacious and cheery, and acted as decisively as ever, refreshed by the fast motoring and a fleeting spring rain, which sprinkled his peaked cap and new olive-colored service jacket, where the order of Saint Vladimir, granted to him for his audacious flights over Turkish artillery batteries, hung on a ribbon over his left pocket, its crimson enamel gleaming.

Without questioning Annushka, who didn't even recognize him in her delirium (there were birth throes after all: the Greek was mistaken there!), he quickly hurried off somewhere in the car, which hadn't even had time to cool down, returning soon with Uncle Josya (the future traitor), a basket of flowers, and an under-officer from General Baklanov's seventeenth Cossack regiment. This under-officer, who'd studied at the military medic school at one time and then agreed to become a covert accoucheur, happened to be Uncle Pavel's brother-in-law, though he was more than a brother-in-law: many photographs, in which the officer usually sits very decorously on a bentwood chair as Uncle Pavel stands with his hand on the other's shoulder, are tenderly and tellingly inscribed, "With Sashenka, brother of my soul." Owing to his rapturous admiration for, and very warm attachment to Uncle Pavel, the under-officer even tried to resemble him in appearance, despite being significantly younger: he had just as huge a Victor Emmanuel mustache, which didn't, however, quite suit his angular face, and he laughed exactly like Uncle

Pavel, with a real "o–ho ho"—opening his mouth wide and rounding his eyes. The fact that under-officer Sashenka had recently lost his right forearm up to the elbow—as he told the story, with wonderment, the arm had suddenly spun away, all by itself, into the thick, vibrating air, flying forward twenty *sazhens* and then continuing to roll, bouncing along the trampled grass together with some peaked caps, after the allied *shell fougasse* that accidentally exploded and tore it off had already completed its brief but powerful flight through the German trenches—didn't in the least confound either Uncle Pavel or the under-officer himself, who'd promised that, despite lacking a hand, he would extract the baby and bring it onto God's earth if Pavlusha ordered him to; he'd use his teeth if need be!

The one-handed under-officer did, indeed, turn out to be unusually deft and ingenious. As he confidently commanded Uncle Josya—who brought in towels, sheets, and pitchers of water—Sashenka didn't simply assist the awakened inmate, who'd been utterly disquieted toward morning by currents of impending life and was shoving his damp little head into a world that was suddenly spacious, sweet-smelling in many ways, and filled with all manner of sounds; Sashenka also didn't simply manage to use his nimble fingers to cut and tie off a dull-purple umbilical cord, whose final action was to spray life-giving juices: he also contrived to hold a slippery little body the color of a baked apple in midair by the feet and measure it with a ribbon one *arshin* long (the baby came to nearly twelve *vershoks*—twelve times the length from one's fingertip to one's second knuckle).

The Immortal One usually did all that: he'd come to love delivering Annushka's babies himself and feeling all the uncles with his own hands when they first came into the world. He'd even taken some of them off to the house's eastern rooms for a time, returning them to Annushka later, all decked out in tiny Cossack cavalry general uniforms. The little uncles had only a short while to sport those tiny uniforms, which were lavishly decorated with braiding, glistening buckles, red edging, and other vivid signs of valorous self-sacrifice. As soon as their parent took his leave from Annushka's bedroom, content with the overall geniality that had welcomed the newly minted cavalrymen into the house, Annushka immediately took those "woolen coats of armor," as she called them, off the infants and cut them to rags without a thought, leaving only little copper sables, and epaulettes with large, faceted stars for the uncles' amusement. "You shouldn't do that, Mamasha," scolded Uncle Seraphim, who'd once detected something very touching and significant in the tiny uniforms. Sometimes he would take small pieces of fabric that had already gotten grease-stained in the kitchen, diligently smoothing them out on his knees as he sat facing her ("Just like a district police officer," she would say) and asking from time to time, "Do you un-derstand what this is? Do you?"

Insulted, she replied—not to Uncle Seraphim himself, but to his golden spectacles, which were thin, narrow to an extreme, and ra-diated an invariable squint of inquisitiveness—that she understood only one thing: Uncle Seraphim had obviously developed a taste for this scratchy foulness and that he most likely shouldn't have been dressed in little white cotton baby undershirts back in the day.

"No, it is not foulness! It is not foulness!" He would suddenly begin hollering, turning crimson. "They are touching signs of atten-tion emanating from the hidden depths of a long-mute heart! That's what they are, Mamasha! … Symbóls! Symbóls!" he would add, al-ready calming down and instantly falling into a reverie at the sound of his very most beloved of words.

"at word really, truly, was nothing more than sound for An-nushka. As with the rhetorical devices Uncle Semyon used in his tirades—some affectedly complex oxymoron or other, fraught with unintelligible duality (Uncle Josya's "stately baseness," or that very same uncle's "noble underhandedness")—the word only perplexed, and sometimes disquieted her if Uncle Seraphim repeated it too fre-quently. Annushka simply couldn't discern the contents—the imper-ishable soul of meaning—of every single word the Creator had con-trived. And no matter how much Uncle Seraphim tried, no matter how much dreaminess and reverie accompanied his utterances of that word, with his echoingly extended pronunciation and exulting, regal "oh," in Annushka's imagination, "symbols" (and only her im-agination, of course, had the power to master that sonorous emptiness, filling it with chance but vivid pictures) conjured up nothing specific and nothing enduring for her until Uncle Seraphim hit upon the idea of declaring none other than Malach himself not only a symbol but, in fact, an eternal and many-faceted symbol!

"Now, there is a symból of wisdom and love, valor and mercy, and the everlastingness of life," he exclaimed again and again, each time the dust-covered and cobweb-wrapped Malach—who was not only fairly withered, but fundamentally fossilized from the lengthy duration of his existence—was extracted, either from underneath the monstrous coffin-like tub that Annushka had, decisively and for all time, doomed to roam dark corners and closets, depriving it of the rank of a utile implement, for the reason that it emitted an abominable drone and loathsomely shuddered upon the very slightest of motions; or out from underneath the graceful French alder divan ("the work, perhaps, of Fourdinois or even, son, Jacob himself!") that had suddenly ended up, for some reason or other, in Uncle Semyon's disfavor after flaunting itself in a visible spot in his office for a long time, or visiting his dressing room more than once, like some important lady, along with a huge, earthenware wood grouse from Annushka's bedroom, which now shared a fate with all the out-of-favor and maimed occupants of Malach's little storage room, where fattened Scolopendrae, gigantic spiders, and, even, according to Uncle Pavel's tales, snakes, greatly enjoyed taking up residence!

They removed Malach fairly often from his storage room (after, that is, he'd been located there), for general viewings in the hexagonal hall: on the older uncles' birthdays, for Easter, and for Christmas. And if those holiday removals drove Uncle Seraphim to a state of exceptional invigoration, unfailingly accompanied as they were by an enterprising and rapturous throng around the "symbol," who was detached from the whole affair and the animated (occasionally overly animated) but mild arguments regarding how and where to position him—perhaps lying, perhaps reclining on a wide settee so he wouldn't, perish the thought, tumble to the floor, or perhaps sitting, after all (certainly sitting, since Annushka had invited a photographer, that priggish Kikiani, and they'd feel thoroughly awkward around him) on the squat and solid Hambs chair with the thickly tufted back where The

Immortal One sat last time, though that chair had now, as if out of spite, gone missing, and the bentwood chair was completely inappropriate because the bentwood had rickety legs, etcetera, etcetera, on and on, until the arrival of the crafty Kikiani, who unexpectedly showed up with two taciturn assistants and of course caught the whole family off guard—well, Uncle Semyon was thrown into such despair by "the insane removals of the unholy idol," as he put things, that he lacked the strength to utter a single word, despite a torturous desire to give vent to his feelings through either menacing prophesies or fiery invective. After placing his hands behind his back and bowing his head, he would withdraw to his office with quick steps even before Kikiani's arrival and is, thus, absent from those numerous holiday photographs in which all the uncles wear white tuxedoes with boutonnières on their satin lapels, in which Annushka wears a ruffled silk dress and a triple strand of pearls, in which the elderly Porphiry is filled with pride and concern as he carefully holds Izmail, over whom aging held no power (and who wouldn't even agree to take off his cap with the feather for a quick minute, though generous Uncle Pavel promised him a silver ruble and a hussar's *sa-bretache*), and in which the imperishable resident of the very most cluttered of little storage rooms solemnly sits on a Hambs chair—the chair, saints be praised, turned up after all!—wearing a huge, tall, lambskin *papakha* on his head and not yet accustomed to the unex-pectedly bright expanses of the festive hall, after his abrupt extrac-tion from cobwebby gloom.

Uncle Semyon deliberately chose not to close his office door. He most likely needed Annushka and all the uncles to hear him play, in doleful solitude, the Austrian glass armonica that an heir to Serbia's throne had once given Uncle Mokei as a reward for his brilliant finishes at the Belgrade horse races. Uncle Semyon had flawlessly mastered this outlandish instrument so completely unneeded by "Mokei Man-drykin, cavalry sergeant-major of the Don Cossack Host and victor of the hippodromes honoring the Kara! or! evi" dynasty" (such was the inscription on the cover). Skillfully pressing the pedals and touching the evenly revolving glass hemispheres with his moistened fingertips, Uncle Semyon forced the armonica to issue unusually melodious, sad, and spectrally melting sounds. They carried through the entire northern section of the house, while Kikiani, as morose and taciturn as his twin assistants, who wore identical cranberry redingotes and golden mustaches, rearranged the uncles from place to place, haughtily and efficiently straightening their pocket-watch chains or crisp shirt bosoms, which glowed like the moon, smoothing someone's overly fluffy side-whisker with the back of a palm, and even attempting (this was utterly discourteous) to slightly raise Uncle Nestor's chin, which had thoroughly slipped to the side and become very, very firmly stuck to his left clavicle after a fragmentation wound in the "glorious, fiery, and merry" ("That's all I remember about it, son!") Battle of Galicia.

Preparations for the magical action of the mechanism contained within a camera from the Freland trading company lasted quite some time. Kikiani apparently found particular enjoyment in dragging out those minutes—they were exhausting for his obedient models, but elating for him—while he still had the power to re-alter something eternity had already overshadowed and to introduce, at his own discretion, sweetly wilful (albeit perhaps insignificant) changes into that sole, inviolable picture predestined for a single indestructible instant in which time has been abruptly taken captive and can move no further than a certain sacred point.

In any event, Kikiani—unlike the cheery, garrulous, and excessively dexterous French photographers, Jacques and Claude, whose insistent appeals in the advertising section of *The Southern Telegraph* "to delight in the refined well-manneredness of the successors of the optician Chevalier" occasionally resonated in Annushka's trusting heart—was in no hurry to remove the massive cover from the lens and use it to sketch his miracle-working circle in the air. (Did he take an elusive moment eternally captive with that quick and surprisingly smooth motion?) It's also possible that the unthinkable may have once occurred, thanks to Kikiani's dawdling. At the last moment, when the capricious photographer, inspired and satisfied at long last with the quivering stillness of everything contained in that huge hall, including Uncle Nestor's fickle chin, which had been raised three fingers higher, at the cost of great effort, and appeared to be pressing an unseen violin to Uncle Nestor's shoulder, had hidden himself under the dark cloth, Uncle Semyon emerged from his office ...

Oh, of course, of course, holy hermits! He emerged not because he'd been possessed with the temptation of coming before the camera's eye in a new velvet *veston* and foppish striped trousers, not at all, but only to search the walnut whatnot cabinet for a special brush to remove dust from the glass armonica. And if he finally came around to being photographed in the company of the uncles—and, even more importantly, in the company of the idol—he certainly did not do so right way, not suddenly, and not of his own will, but only following the lengthy persuasion, and finally the insistence of Annushka, who'd entreated him with the solemnity of the holiday of the Radiant Resurrection of Christ to refrain from dreary seclusion and wearisome music-making. And thus it occurred that this Easter photograph was one of a kind—out beyond its borders no sound could be heard from the glass armonica, which the musician had abandoned in the endless, unportrayed expanse, forever separated from the stately, clear picture by invincible boundaries, as if it were the territory of a vast state apart from a small but unconquerable enclave fraught with impassivity—for in that photograph, Uncle Semyon is standing in the very center. He even found strength within himself (and this may be most surprising of all) to submit to a request from Kikiani, who suddenly wanted Uncle Semyon to touch Malach's shoulder as if in an outburst of filial love, but not with all five fingers, like Uncle Pavel, who was wont to taking protective stances toward the people caught in sitting positions alongside him during such radiant photographic moments, but only with the tip of his ring finger ... Yes, yes, like that: according to Kikiani's scheme, Uncle Semyon should exquisitely, naturally, and also emotionally and deferentially, touch Malach's shoulder. But Kikiani apparently missed something. Preoccupied with establishing order among an ever-changing array of secondary details on the flanks, he hadn't noticed the treacherous inaccuracies that came about as if by stealth in the very center of the polysyllabic and majestic hieroglyph of familial cohesion and unwavering geniality he'd so laboriously created, a place where Uncle Semyon's figure was a sign of no small importance. He hadn't noticed, for example, that Uncle Semyon had stepped a half-stride away from the chair and then leaned back slightly, that he'd carelessly placed his left foot too far forward and much too far away, and, furthermore, the right hand he'd decisively placed on his waist made his velvet *veston* bulge jauntily and provocatively on his side. In short, Kikiani hadn't noticed a crucial point: thanks to those significant and undoubtedly artistic trifles, the touch turned out to be not at all heartfelt and bashful, but closer to cold and demanding: Uncle Semyon proudly looks off to the side, holds his left arm, ornamented by a bracelet, over the back of the chair, and testily waits for it to finally dawn on them (on whom? maybe on Kikiani's assistants, stationed with the lighting equipment at the very borders of this sovereign immobility; or on Annushka's ever-unsober steward, who had suddenly appeared in the hall with both a *shtof* bottle that had already been largely emptied and the firm intention of kissing the photographer gentleman in celebration of Easter; or maybe on the photographer himself) to remove the repulsive object his ring finger had long pointed at.

Of course, Uncle Semyon subsequently tormented himself severely for this compulsory contact. He spoke about it as the most peccant and most unlikely action of his life, moreover he demanded from the archangels and seraphs rapid retribution for himself with such inconsolability and such prayerful ardor that if they hadn't been all-knowing, they might have thought Uncle Semyon had, at the very least, danced in Hell with Satan on Holy Easter. The photograph itself, however, which Kikiani prepared the next day and delivered immediately by courier (Jacques and Claude's Easter photographs always came, at best, only toward the conclusion of St. Thomas Week), not only pleased Uncle Semyon, but, over time, even became for him the object of constant delight and dreamy contemplation. There were two explanations for this: first, Uncle Semyon found, and not exactly without reason, that he was dazzlingly magnificent in the photograph. Second, he couldn't remain indifferent after Uncle Pavel made a very important observation, or perhaps even an extraordinary discovery, on Seraphim's birthday. As Uncle Pavel drank a cup of coffee and paged through a hefty photo album covered in dark-green velour and decorated for some reason with the raised figure of a ballerina (a photographer sporting a mustache, vest, and the essential boater would have been far more apropos), he remarked aloud that in this photograph Uncle Semyon bore an uncommon resemblance to his fervent parent.

There's no need to say that this remark held exceptional importance and strength in Uncle Semyon's eyes, since it was uttered at a moment of familial celebration, when The Immortal One was within the circle of his sons, and since Uncle Pavel was the only one, besides Annushka and one madcap female in-law, who had actually laid eyes on the Greek and who, consequently, could confirm that the splendid Greek, the inspired Greek—ah, it's finally time, yes, it's time to give his name, Antipatros—that the Antipatros whom Annushka had assured the uncles "was invented by Syomushka from head to toe," therein exasperating her secretly born son with her cunning absentmindedness, did exist after all. There's also no need to say that this remark heartened Uncle Semyon, stoking his imagination and touching him so much that he was prepared to forgive the perfidious Uncle Pavel all his offenses that very minute; the Pavel who had more than once, in Annushka and Malach's presence, renounced his own heated testimonials by insisting more than once that he'd never met the mysterious Greek, either in the circus tent with wondrous stars sewn all over it, fluttering in the wind, or in the little square by the Host's clerical office, where a sparkly, dispersed light emanated from the window of the *sotnik* on duty, illuminating the crowns of summer lindens until the first sounds were heard from a nimble broom and an unhurried morning horsecar; or in any other place whatsoever. "For the Greek," Uncle Pavel swore to the Holy Mother of God, "is an impossible figure, fantastical in the highest degree."

It ought to be specially noted, however, that one vexing circumstance did cloud Uncle Semyon's joy: referring to the Greek could no longer incense, rattle, or even bewilder The Immortal One. This was a time when he had not yet been deprived of his hearing but had lost the ability to distinguish the sounds of speech from other, less significant and less intricate sounds, (a fly's buzz or a door's squeak), and, after that, alas, also the ability to express himself intelligibly. Of the great abundance of words known to The Immortal One at one time and now hopelessly forgotten, his memory had retained only the tenderly murmuring word "giraffe" and "welland-welland," which nobody understood. Admittedly, Uncle Seraphim appeared to have no great difficulty understanding that strange "welland-welland." At Christmas, for example, as it happened—when they were readying themselves for the arrival of the unfailingly gloomy Kikiani, or the ever noisy and affable Jacques and Claude, with a particular excitement that was growing in proportion to the joyfully complex and sweet Christmas aroma that had filled the house since morning and was gaining strength and becoming more and more apparent and dizzying as it offered solos from, in turn, sappy evergreen needles, which mellowed in the warm residence, hot apple pastries, parquet floor cleaned with pistachio polish, or cool, damp mandarin oranges—Malach, who'd been triumphantly extracted from his little storage room early in the morning and forgotten by everyone for some time, suddenly grasped at Uncle Seraphim's sleeve as the uncle hurried toward the site of the photography shoot (the western part of the hexagonal hall) with some sort of "capital" decree and pointed at a tall spruce with sagging, flat boughs, exclaiming, "Welland-welland!"

And Uncle Seraphim—displaying his wonderful ability to instantly understand the very sincere, complex, and varied something that emanated from the "mysterious depths of a long-muted heart," and was shackled to the very same sounds that may have been chance and irrational but had caught Malach's fancy for some reason—responded infallibly and immediately to that enthusiastic but also demanding outburst in which a less keen ear might have heard, perhaps, only surprise and delight at a sumptuously decorated fir, or an unintended eruption of vaguer feelings but, of course, nothing resembling what the highly sagacious Uncle Seraphim heard. Without thinking for even a minute, as if Malach had stated his unusual wish—and, fathers of eloquence, he had, incidentally, stated exactly that: a wish!—with the most common of words, Uncle Seraphim quickly and randomly took everything from the fir branches that was at hand: a silver-plated sphere; garlands of glass beads; a bunch of golden metal ornaments; a little cardboard angel with a bugle; and a small, cotton shepherd thickly sprinkled with glass dust; and just as quickly used those objects, all of them inexplicably touching in their fleeting holiday splendor, to decorate the carefree prisoner of deepest longevity, who nodded to him, greeting him with a grateful smile, and then entered a lengthy, silent, and blissful placidity.

And that's how The Immortal One sits in that year's Christmas photograph: meekly happy, beaming, and "decked out," as Annushka expressed it, "more beautifully than a Christmas tree." That photograph, incidentally, reveals to a greater degree than others the independence of its own internal, inexhaustive life from the refined luminoscribe's calculations and schemes, from, at the very least, the dazzling effect of the final artillerist's gesture that Kikiani made after bursting out from underneath the dark cloth in a vain attempt to avert unintended poses, unconstrained motions, or involuntary facial expressions within the detailed picture he'd conceptualized. Uncle Nestor used a similar gesture (since artillery has already been mentioned here) while commanding a squadron in the Battle of Galicia and thwarting audacious Austro-Hungarian cavalry counterattacks with heroic mercilessness: gesturing to forewarn before a harsh "Fire!", or a heartfelt "For our Serbian brothers!", until one day a shard from a shell fougasse suddenly stopped screeching under his overcoat, even though it hadn't yet completed its breakneck flight, hadn't upended him from a high glacis, and hadn't carried him off, as Uncle Nestor remembered it, "straight through the air" in the direction of Lutsk, over blindages and foxholes, over cooling shell craters, over the thrown-back heads of young cannoneers, who hadn't yet been drawn into the majestic battle and thus regarded Uncle Nestor with wary curiosity (one of them, oh, that scamp! even found time to salute after catching sight of the little stars on Uncle Nestor's field epaulettes), over a little lake and ravine, over a fallen aeroplane, over a medic tent, around which a corpulent doctor wearing a comfortable *bekishe* over his smock and only one boot, which happened to be splotched with clay, zealously chased after a concussed bombardier, and, finally, over the uninhabited and peacefully blooming plain, above which Uncle Nestor had been flying for so surprisingly long a time and in so completely a carefree fashion, he'd already forgotten the harmonious cannons that had cheerily roared upon his command, and the Austro-Hungarian cavalry blindly milling around in a sea of dust, and everything else on earth, and was blissfully tumbling and freely soaring toward the sunny heavens along with his map case and foppish cane.

Now Uncle Nestor uses that walrus tusk cane to move Uncle Alexander's foot—slightly and with delicate insistence—away from his own polished and decorously shining shoe, not paying the slightest attention to the photographer's decisive gesture, just as Uncle Alexander pays no attention to that gesture and has unexpectedly turned his head to tell Uncle Nestor his arguments as obligingly and amiably as possible: in the first place Porphiry is crowding him, teetering heavily from side to side and unintentionally bumping everyone around him because he's holding Uncle Izmail, who's fidgety, crankily bent, and agitated because they'd taken away his Cuirassier sword, dulled though it is but dangerous nevertheless in the hands of a feeble-minded elder infant (Annushka never determined who'd taken the sword from the wall and given it to Izmail); in the second place, Uncle Nestor had enough space to his left to move slightly further away from Uncle Alexander if he really couldn't allow his unquestionably refined and even splendid shoe to neighbor Uncle Alexander's crude boot; and in the third place (this being the most important), Uncle Nestor shouldn't imagine that his heroic maiming—which, as it happens, Uncle Alexander thinks could have been avoided if, let's say, Uncle Nestor hadn't found such particular pleasure in rakishly standing in ostentatious poses on all manner of mounds, small hills, and other picturesque rises, as if for paintings—that this dramatic maiming gave him the right to obnoxiously jab at Uncle Alexander's foot with an outlandish cane that he needed (there was no argument there); and furthermore, as Uncle Nestor was aware, he was jabbing a foot that wasn't real but lovingly and masterfully prepared by Alfred von Winkler of Luxembourg to replace a nimble, light, and joyfully imperceptible foot he'd "unwittingly lost in the Caucasian theater of war in 1915," under generally everyday circumstances, building viaducts across a ravine, because of some arrogant riflemen's insignificant maneuver. Uncle Pavel doesn't notice the photographer's signal and has decided to pull his hand out of his pocket after all, though he doesn't have quite enough time to place it on Seraphim's shoulder, and Uncle Josya has entirely devoted himself to combating a persistent tormenter, a yawn as supple as an under-ripe lemon (and already half-quashed in his mouth). In short, the photograph turned out to look so spontaneous that if a cheery, dapper man-about-town in a striped suit and unmatched vest hadn't been playing tricks at the back of the photograph by unfurling seven elegantly inscribed letters over his head like a flying fan

one might have thought it had been hastily snapped by Jacques and Claude, who weren't accustomed to crudely interfering in "l'ordre naturel des choses,"[2] as they were in the habit of explaining things to Annushka, adroit as they were, though overly theatrical in their imitation of artists whose lofty feelings had been hurt, and deliberately switching to French when she pointed out the obvious slip-ups in their "improvisation éclatante"[3] in an attempt to limit payment for the photograph to only the deposit. Kikiani stuck to a different rule, justifiably thinking "l'ordre naturel des choses" didn't always create a beneficial impression on a nitpicking customer like Annushka, who had changed family luminoscribes with unusual enthusiasm before settling one day on Kikiani; this meant the level of his painstaking art couldn't sink to the slipshod hastiness typical of Jacques and Claude. If he'd sunk to their level anyway, it was likely from despair that the picture—well-proportioned, and, at some moment, already complete, in his fastidious view—had been horned in on

---

2 The natural order of things (French)

3 Splendid improvisation (French)

by more and more new characters who'd used foresight in amassing benches, chairs, and stands, and unexpectedly expressed their wish to immortalize their holiday miens by stepping onto the territory of a fantastical land, a gleaming island ready to become, a minute later, a stronghold of delightful permanence in an ocean of inconstant images and fluid time.

There was only one way for Kikiani to stop the secondary figures from piling up: raise his arm, hurriedly remove the cap from the lens, and seize what might not have been the most fitting moment. That decision, at any rate, relieved him of the necessity of bickering with Annushka, whose decree permitted the Christmas photograph to include not only all the uncles' wives and daughters-in-law but all manner of bull-headed brothers-in-law and tin-pot sons-in-law, as well as all those countless relations-by-marriage who trudged around behind Porphiry, having grown attached to him, harum-scarum, back in the days of his devil-may-care youth when he'd eagerly organized legendary carousing sessions resplendent with a variety of victuals and generous gifts—a foal for one, a Derbent rug for another, an *astrakhan* hat for a third—never suspecting that in his old age, close to his demise, after they'd assiduously fleeced him, he would seriously, and not as a joke, as he had earlier, think from time to time about the hurdy-gurdy, meaning, as he'd dreamily said when intoxicated during times of ravishing abundance, he was considering heading for the streets with a beggar's bag, a hurdy-gurdy, and Izmail the dancer.

"Yes, yes, the streets! The streets!" he would repeat, looking around a house that echoed more than usual and had meekly brightened. He was repeating this, of course, not with the forced beggar's woe that had been unfamiliar to him, the woe that had, at one time, evoked unctuous giggles among his tipsy, tightfisted kin at his name-day parties, but rather with the sincere, brisk, and nervously cheery decisiveness of a wealthy man gone bankrupt: "Shall we hit the streets, dear Izmail? Shall we?"

To which Izmail would melodiously honk an expression of exuberant agreement, puffing out his rosy cheeks and gesturing wildly, or would suddenly grab the chair with the black, singed seat, the only chair the discerning daughters-in-law didn't covet: he would hold the chair in front of himself, lean back, and comically stride through the rooms, impersonating an overly dashing and happy-go-lucky hurdy-gurdy man.

Uncle Porphiry tended to amuse himself by contemplating a hurdy-gurdy (something that, as it happened, he'd never owned) more often than by dreaming of using his apiary capital to knock together a small flour mill in his picturesque *stanitsa*, which was crisscrossed with little streams, or to build an opulent bakery—most certainly with divans and stained glass—somewhere in the city, on Arsenal Street perhaps, for the gentlemen officers. This inclination toward tragic destitution that accompanied his unhurried but un-failing—thanks to the inexhaustible beehives—accumulation of wealth sometimes possessed him with such strength that, despite his reputation for a deferential relationship with Annushka, and a charming rural sedateness (not at all acquired, as it happened, from the effects of sweet-smelling air and serenity induced by long hours of labor, as certain of the uncles assumed, but rather from the in-come-bearing stocks of some mysterious Istrin Sawmill Company, which flourished fantastically in the treeless plains), he couldn't re-frain from theatrical behaviors that drove poor Annushka to faints. Tales were told, for example, of how he suddenly appeared before her in the middle of the night—as if he'd come from the officers' club—dressed in a chalk-spotted *beshmet* and with intentionally disheveled side-whiskers, collapsed on the floor and rolled around, shouting in an unnatural voice that he was destitute!—destitute because that night at the billiard table ("Oh yes! At the billiard table, Mamenka! Blast it thrice!") he'd thrown to the wind not only all his money, the estate, and the hives, but also Malach's house, God forgive him.

"They tore me to pieces, to pieces, the crooks! They sent me to the poorhouse! Killed me!" he exclaimed, heated and reveling in the woeful meaning of those phony words. "I'm going to live as a beggar, Mamenka! Do you hear? Starting tomorrow! With the hurdy-gurdy! …"

He would often come by toward evening, too, mightily unsober and grandly gloomy, call for the steward, who was even more unsober but also blissfully cheery, and (without even going inside) entrust the steward with reciting for the lady of the house a dramatically muddled story of his "decisive and colossal" downfall, a story that grew more complicated each time and amounted to the following, if the inconsistent details are tossed aside. Some cunning and ill-intentioned scoundrel ("Lousy little huckster! Whoremonger!") had bought up in large quantity promissory notes allegedly issued by Uncle Porphiry and totaling a fabulous sum, and then, of course, presented them, with nefarious abruptness, for collection, right then and there; at the same time other notes that Uncle Porphiry had, for his part, bought up with no malice whatsoever (albeit, perhaps, with the intent of some modest income) had all turned out to be thoroughly counterfeit, meaning all the men-about-town and dandies who'd passed them off as mythical wealth had long been rattling around in fetters, and since Uncle Porphiry had hoped to extinguish his notes at the expense of the notes from the men-about-town and dandies, and since the huckster-whoremonger had no desire of hearing about any deferrals, well then, Uncle Porphiry could be rattling around in fetters any day now, too.

"So, you tell her," he instructed the steward, who, to please Uncle Porphiry, had instantly sobered up and even become gloomy, "they'll put Porphiry in fetters! ... Parade him around the city!"

Uncle Pavel, however, told the most ludicrous and outrageous story. He insisted he'd once seen Uncle Porphiry holding out his hat on the parvis of the Cossack Host's cathedral: Uncle Porphiry was apparently got up in such horribly pitiful puttees, and wailing "Donate in the name of Christ!" with such stricken grief, as he widely opened his lopsided, suffering mouth and looked off into the heavens, that even the cripples and beggars who flocked around him from all sides (despite those puttees, according to Uncle Pavel, Uncle Porphiry stood out amongst them like Samson among the Philistine hordes, thanks to his patriarchally powerful figure and full-blooded facial flora), consoled him by placing what they had in the hat, be it a copper or a sweet roll.

It's entirely possible that at some point Uncle Porphiry would have savored that genuine poverty to which his soul aspired—perhaps drawn by Providence—but alas! (or fortunately?) his dozen surviving beehives, and the bees' tenacious and foolhardy industriousness reliably protected him from it in his final years. It's also possible that at some point he might also have decided, in a burst of undying yearning for a beggar's fate, to sell his honey-rich hives for a song to the sensible miser of a neighbor, or the importunate distiller with the outlandishly combed beard who'd visited him once a week, to bargain for them with either restrained enterprise or a skinflint's frenzy. It also cannot be ruled out that Uncle Porphiry might have used the banknotes he'd earned—whether from a neighbor or a distiller—to finally acquire an obediently chittering hurdy-gurdy imbued with clear, crystalline, and hopelessly repetitious sounds ("most certainly German-made, my dear Izmailushka!") and set off into the streets with it after all, his tragic baritone belting out coyly passionate and falsely sorrowful little songs about unfortunate love—maybe of a lame fourrier for a haughty sutler girl who was the secret daughter of a count and a lay-about woman, or maybe of a hunch-backed sutler girl for a highfalutin fourrier, a handsome man and bon vivant—about all sorts of convicts' and orphans' unenviable lots, about lives poisoned early, about someone's bull-headed sadness, and so on and so on, all of it bitingly soulful and peskily doleful, all of which he would have sung about with pent-up agitation, quenching a long-standing thirst in his heart and, perhaps, accompanied by Uncle Izmail's incongruously dashing, squatting dances.

Of course, if Uncle Porphiry had decided on these squalid escapades—on this "licentious panhandling," as Uncle Semyon might have exclaimed in a fit of oratorical inspiration—he wouldn't have been stopped by either Annushka's tears or the reproaches of Uncle Seraphim, who was well-informed regarding the value of the *stanitsa* property ("Even if it's second rate, my dear Porphiry! Even if it's neglected!"), which Uncle Porphiry was quite capable of burning up in order to free himself once and for all and not trouble with property, and, even more likely, in order to have the bitter inspiration that a humble, conscientiously miserable beggar with a hurdy-gurdy so needed. He could scarcely have been stopped by stern cautions from Uncle Pavel, who would have blustered (admittedly primarily for the sake of witticism) that he would curtail this unprecedented

buffoonery right then and there, using whatever methods neces-
sary—meaning he wouldn't helplessly throw his hands up in the air
and shake his head in grief, like Uncle Josya or Uncle Alexander; he
would instead buy off some village constable or other, if he had to,
to promptly capture the rowdy duet, secure them in Malach's home
with the help of a saber, and confiscate the inseparable artists' hurdy-
gurdy—may it be thrice cursed!—and knapsack containing spice
cookies given as alms. No, Uncle Porphiry had always been character-
ized by a frenzied, buoyant wilfulness, which gained momentum as
the bee families in his sturdy, fir hives expanded and multiplied—a
living, tireless substance thickened there, its seething froth impetuously gushing out the hive entrance into sultry May noontides—and
his well-tended bit of capital increased, too, "fleshed out," as he liked
to state it, diligently fattening its flanks in a quiet, respectable bank;
he also never lost his fervent wilfulness, even in the days of pen-
niless, meager old age. Quite the contrary, quite the contrary! According to Annushka's observations, her mighty and autocratic firstborn, who'd suddenly and enigmatically come to love all manner of
shabbiness—perplexed, she reasoned this was either from untimely
prosperity or an excessively heart-felt union with the unfortunate Izmail—had grown even more impulsive in his old age, and even more
unbending, taking cockamamie decisions and actions that every now
and again fully astonished their decorous kith and kin, courteous
neighbors, the officers' club (which had certainly seen everything),
and the humble Club for All Social Classes, where he went every
Wednesday to content himself with the gramophone and something
low-key and low stakes. He even astounded Uncle Izmail, whose
mind was detached from all manner of earthly woes and invulner-
able to sorrowful deliberations, but still filled (judging from his
dashing dancing) with agonizing unease: Izmail's guardian, for example, once suddenly returned home from the city toward morning
with a huge and indecently sumptuous coffin he'd purchased—not
as it happened, seeing it, after some sober and gloomy reckoning, as
a doleful necessity, but rather from bravado—on a buffoonish im-
pulse during a debauched auction that raged all night in an eating establishment under the leadership of a drunken *mortus*. The thought,

by the way, that Uncle Izmail's despondency exerted a pernicious influence on his elder brother was raised more than once, and not only by Annushka. Those very same daughters-in-law, sisters-in-law, and scathing sons-in-law who'd eagerly sung along with everything and who had, at one time, very rashly and unceremoniously implicated Uncle Porphiry (he, the very kindest of the uncles, oh, you insidious sorcerers!) in "clouding" the baby's clear powers of reason with mead and pursuing the evil goal of turning Izmail into a monster and a mad sentinel of Porphiry's village holdings, took it upon themselves to harp, as a unified voice, on something that wasn't completely palatable, but was, nevertheless, essentially the exact opposite. They painstakingly acted out for Annushka fits of the tenderest concern for her eldest son's whims, saying that Uncle Porphiry, pressured by an ill-starred fate that had doomed him to survive placidly aging children and grandchildren who'd tasted of longevity, and, of course, reed-thin wives with rickety health (who, however, we will note in passing, had still managed to besiege him with cohesive cohorts of imperishable sisters-in-law), and who had taken upon himself the overwhelming burden of raising Izmail, who, according to their new-found deductive reasoning, became a lunatic even before his conception—yes, yes, they were seers!—even back within those mysterious realms, those halls of the Everlasting where each Likeness forms, from whence the past and that to come are mercilessly expelled, as if from an orderly kingdom in an age-old photograph; they maintained that, toward the end of Uncle Porphiry's life, after having learned so well how to understand his insane brother, he constantly entered the dark labyrinths of madness with his luminous mind, too, and partially went out of his own head. And if that inadvertent madness he'd caught ("Caught!" they confidently said, as if they were talking about a head cold or scabies) from Uncle Izmail hadn't driven him to utter mental laxity or an idiotic crouching dance—in fact, when Uncle Porphiry was in a cheerful disposition, he quite eagerly crouched and could even outdance Uncle Izmail, which distressed the latter to tears—it was only due to the healthy society of vigilant relatives by marriage who were always bestowing their salutary presence on Porphiry.

And, indeed, Uncle Porphyry knew no loneliness as long as he had something to live off, and as long as his numerous larders—palaces of aromatic chilliness, where a radiantly bright, flowing product languished in alder barrels in expectation of foodstuff markets and out-of-town wholesale merchants—had not turned to bastions of fetor or the habitual abodes of spiders and rats; until his gardens, immense vegetable beds, and vast flower plantings withered away; and until a painfully lonely clarity and a marvelous, majestically beautiful immobility (undeniable signs of impoverishment) could be detected even above his estate in the very air, air that had once been a cloudy amber and suffused with a vehement, productive vibration. Among the few, but very reliable and soulful joys that accompanied the ruin that came to favor him was the possibility of secluded and peaceful living, as well as the possibility of aimlessly roaming the estate in indescribably shabby underwear or an intact silver bandolier he wore along with a much-loved *beshmet*, which was donned directly onto his naked body and was still fairly dapper. Of course that ruin befell him not as his heart had demanded, meaning not at once, not suddenly, and not with the fatal abruptness of a stunning wreck. No, unlike the "devilish," "monstrous," or "grandiose" ruin that fell smack upon him in his persistent dreams, his real-life ruin befell him with the same favorable leisureliness affected by an affectionate compeer— a police chief who once came to arrest him for an impudent escapade in regional court ("Well, well, you prankster, we've been ordered to take you!"); the officer didn't neglect to sample, along the way, some young wine and aromatic brined vegetables in his most cordial dining companion's cellars. Even so, this commonplace circumstance—that his wealth, which had quietly floated away, part of it misappropriated, part of it given away, but most of it stolen—did not altogether prevent Porphyry from anguishing over the wealth as if it had disappeared instantly as the result of a devastating billiards loss, or perhaps an underhanded huckster's cunning operation. As he strolled through the house, aimlessly looking into monotonously bright rooms whose emptying had required neither months nor years but entire decades from prudent in-laws who'd initially shunned theft as being too perceptible and unceremonious—it was only later that they fleeced the uncle with an unabashed and joyous fascination that turned to malicious thrill-seeking toward the end—Uncle Porphiry suddenly began stamping his foot, fell to the floor as he'd done some time ago in Annushka's bedroom, and woefully burst out, "A disaster, my dear Izmail! Devastating! The hurdy-gurdy! ..."

In short, it seemed Uncle Porphiry would make his dream of the hurdy-gurdy—of inspired panhandling that he couldn't imagine without that marvelous and indifferently obedient instrument imbued with imperishable sounds, an instrument that appeared to him, of course, to be a symból of genuine impoverishment—a reality, come what may. But his demise, a demise that found him in the attic early one morning, repairing the chimney, doomed that frenzied dream never to come true, for all eternity.

Uncle Porphiry's entire estate went irrevocably to seed after his death: it was overgrown with reeds and cattails, deep grass, and impenetrable bushes. Tenacious rivulets invaded the territory later, gravitating toward fetid swamps and emerging lakes: with time they merged into one stream that was broad, snaking, and thickly dotted with tiny islands, and that stream absorbed Uncle Porphiry's boxy house, shrouding it in mire. The stable and outbuilding disappeared without a trace shortly thereafter, and the carriage house disappeared somewhere, most likely vanishing into boggy oblivion by the riverside, or hiding under the crowns of fattened willows. Other structures that may not have been so vast, but were, nevertheless, once fairly noticeable, were also nowhere to be found, either in the swampy floodplain or the ever-moving river islands that were always protruding from or disappearing into the drowsily glistening water. Uncle Izmail got lost somewhere on those islands, too, among the impenetrable vegetation. The endless battles he waged all those years, armed with a lashing cherry branch (and occasionally an Albanian saber from Uncle Porphiry's collection) against various and sundry insects, including those same mysterious, insidious ones that so acutely harmed the bees, freezing both the bees themselves and their radiant honey—those desperate battles most likely took on some sort of special, exceptionally intricate character that demanded clandestine and circumspect action from their adversaries, at least from Uncle Izmail.

He no longer emitted bellicose whoops and didn't sink to a crouch when he exulted in victory during either fleeting battles or drawn-out campaigns. Which is the most likely reason why Izmail couldn't be located after Annushka sent Uncle Pavel out in search of him one unusually droughty summer, despite all Uncle Pavel's long wandering and listening to every rustle along the shallowing stream and the dried-up swamps and growing islands, so very long that giant, shaggy birds with transparent wings resembling bumblebees even appeared before him. They were frightening and nimble, and Uncle Pavel claimed they floated completely noiselessly through the air, circling in huge flocks over his chestnut horse and plotting something hostile, even, more than once, knocking the visored cap from his head after unexpectedly flying out of tall bushes where lurking cicadas incessantly buzzed, intensifying the swooning effect of the summer heat. It was most likely they ("Those very same rascals, Mamenka!" Uncle Pavel insisted) whom Izmail had fought his entire life.

In any event, when Uncle Pavel returned from the *stanitsa*, he decisively announced that he would never go there again, either on horseback, or with a coachman and landaulet, or—even—in the foppish Dux with the booming klaxon horn he'd enjoyed riding around in everywhere and that had played a special role in Uncle Semyon's fate, for it was in that gleaming petromobile—No, God would not forget its exacting creators!—that Uncle Pavel secretly brought under-officer Sashenka, the one-handed accoucheur ("the meek warrior," "the crippled angel," as Uncle Semyon affectionately referred to him) to Malach's house on that windy April night; in short Uncle Pavel had brought an ambassador of fate who wasn't, for some reason, alluded to in Antipatros's prophecy.

In the meantime, Sashenka, an under-officer with light, fan-shaped brows, which were always raised high (which meant an expression of welcoming surprise never left his face), a touching smile, a baby's clear gaze, and a fat, ash-blond mustache, painstakingly cultivated in emulation of Uncle Pavel's, was the first person Uncle Semyon beheld upon entering the world.

The under-officer stood before him in his usual uniform—that of a senior petty officer of General Baklanov's seventeenth Cossack regiment. Of course, the newborn uncle examined that uniform, like the junior officer's face, in all its particulars, and one of those particulars became etched into his memory for the ages. It was a regimental badge: a modest army symb. l that simply testified to the junior officer's attachment to the Baklanov regiment. But Uncle Se-myon never wished to reconcile himself with that "simply." "Because that badge, oh angels," he solemnly proclaimed, gazing upon the chandelier, "flaunted itself not just anywhere, but on the chest of he who met me at the hour of dawn on the threshold of my future life! …"

"And because it is through symbols that Providence articulates itself with people," Uncle Seraphim added, very apropos, as he expressed what happened to be an unrelated thought.

And it must be acknowledged that the badge was fairly singular, unlike other regimental badges, where numerals predominate. This badge depicts—Lord have mercy!—a human skull and crossbones, framed by this caption:

I await the resurrection of the dead and the life of the world to come. Amen.

PART III
THE STORAGE ROOM

Annushka had a horrifying dream a few days after she had been safely delivered of the baby with the help of under-officer Sashenka: Malach Grigorevich, fraught with menacing fury, was galloping on a huge, mud-spattered horse and holding a pike, atilt. And on that pike—holy, holy!—were strung the uncles, each and every one of them: those who undeniably already existed at the time and those of whom there was yet no trace, meaning Uncle Petr and Uncle Izmail, whose groundlessly happy faces sprang before Annushka with a wondrous distinctiveness that still awaited capture by the family luminoscribe.

In Uncle Seraphim's interpretation, that dream augured the imminent return of The Immortal One and so it was decided to take baby Syomushka off to the orphanage without delay, according to the Greek's instructions.

Looking furtively around and speaking quietly amongst themselves, Josya, Pavel, and under-officer Sashenka, under cover of night, removed little Semyon from Malach's house hidden in a chest, got into the automobile, together with their secret cargo, and quickly raced off, scattering the air with scarlet sparkles from cigarettes they all lit as they headed toward Trinity Square, where a stout woman already waited by the gates of an orphanage run under the auspices of Prince Cherkesov: she, the orphanage matron, was fully informed about the deceit that was afoot.

The matron met the nocturnal guests with uncommon cordiality, remembering the Greek's generosity in awarding her gold imperials for the promise of providing services to his beloved in this ticklish matter, which Antipatros had summarized using the expression "wrap the old dimwit around your finger." As it happened, however, the matron didn't show even the slightest indication she'd long known one of her guests, that being Uncle Josya, rather intimately. Furthermore, Uncle Semyon alleged that the matron—who seemed endlessly troubled by city reporters' notices that repeatedly claimed, with envious reproach, that the quantity of horseless carriages "had increased incredibly, to the joy of the proprietor of the gasoline station"—had by that time already entertained thoughts of becoming a full-fledged proprietress at The Vulcan's Well. In any event, Uncle Semyon knew for certain that the fat-bottomed gentleman in the leather helmet, double-breasted jacket, and gloves with arm guards, who kept appearing near the gates to the Carriage Market on moonless nights and arousing the curiosity of observant street sweepers, the very same gentleman who always carried a can under his arm, ostensibly for fuel, was the matron. After changing into the cumbersome attire of a chauffeur, and even gluing a huge mustache as black as tar under her nose, she went in that guise to visit Uncle Josya at his gasoline-scented headquarters in an out-of-the-way, hidden room crammed with machine-oil barrels, where she paid her compliments for hours, simultaneously studying his receipts book after craftily asking to view it at just that exciting moment when their compliments (and perhaps seclusion itself) were naturally taking on a frolicsome character. In other words, Uncle Semyon insisted, the matron was already involved in extraordinarily frivolous relations with Josya, which were doubly reprehensible because, in the first place, Josya's spouse, "young but ailing, son," was still alive at the time, meaning the sorrowful fate the seller of combustibles had prepared for her had yet to strike—according to Uncle Semyon's version of the story, Josya insidiously poisoned her, using kerosene to treat his sweet wife's indigestion—and then, in the second place, that the matron, an "irrepressible, fat, giddy woman, my God!" and "brazen comedienne, oh angels!" was not at the midday but in the gloaming of her life … Oh, yes, yes! And the only thing that could be more horrifying than her would have been the hideously swollen, fissured, drowned woman who'd taken it upon herself to constantly strangle poor Uncle Alexander at night, after that time in 1915 or 1916 when he'd nearly lost his life in an unknown tributary of the Tigris, having inadvertently splashed into its murky waters with an entire platoon of pontoniers—those most excellent pontoon builders— with whom he'd parted ways for eternity without announcing any further orders ("The *vodyanoy*—that mean old man of the waters— is your commander now, brothers!") about urgent construction of a structure for a river crossing.

In the shot that appeared in the family photo album two years later, however, after Uncle Josya unexpectedly became a widower and married Felitsia Karpovna (that being the matron's name), she looks to be, contrary to the assurances of her sharp-tongued brother-in-law, a fresh lady who's barely begun to bloom, so very sweet in appearance that even Uncle Pavel's wife, who had a reputation as a wondrous beauty and thus didn't wish to see herself in Christmas photos alongside those "pompous plain things" (as almost all the uncles' spouses, alas, seemed to her) found it within herself to neighbor Felitsia Karpovna, even though the luminoscribe, it must be noted, objected terribly. "You're too slender, dearie! And Felitsia Karpovna is too ample! It would be better for you, my good lady, to take your place right here," Kikiani insisted, indicating a place where now—in that illuminated, unflagging, and placid now that's not subject to the pointlessly eternal inconstancy that rules all and is obediently called time—the slim Lukerya, who's Uncle Alexander's "sweet thorn," stands, alongside the similarly slim Agraphena, who's Uncle Nestor's "Mamochka," both wearing impossibly small hats with nearly indistinguishable little veils lightly sprinkled with beads, and both, as the photographer explained to them, in the first row to slightly conceal the heaviness of a left flank composed of Seraphim Malachovich's substantial sisters-in-law, among whom Felitsia Karpovna often turns up at Kikiani's request.

Of course, the photos prepared by Jacques and Claude do not contain similar, if not fanciful, then certainly deliberate pairings: the gallant brothers Chevalier, the "scions of the great opticist," were consistent in their attempts to reward splendid immobility only to moments "de la vie naturel" that were also resplendent in the refined politesse they tirelessly mentioned time and again in the advertising section of *The Southern Telegraph*. No matter how the gussied-up personages in the luminoscript arranged themselves in front of the new Eastman camera—yes, may that be known to our kind hostess—on which the poor French artistes had expended an entire fortune ("But it izz a wonderful camera obscura, madame!"), no matter what poses the restless uncles' wives took, zealously changing places, and no matter what the already rather unsober brothers-in-law cooked up, officiously swaggering in uniforms strewn with confetti, everything was "pas mal" or even "très bien!" for Jacques and Claude—whether someone sat cross-legged on the floor or embraced Porphiry's wife's sisters. They not only failed to nip comedic actions in the bud, but even seemed to willingly encourage them, particularly Felitsia Karpovna's pranks: she sometimes permitted herself to clown around with uncommon brazenness, meaning her unkind brother-in-law was, indeed, correct. And things impossible to even imagine in the presence of Kikiani—whose sullen efficiency served as an insuperable obstacle even to a harmless lack of inhibition, not to mention jesting—often occurred, as if on their own, when these scatterbrained artists got down to business. Once, for example, they permitted something absolutely unthinkable, perhaps even impertinent. They permitted Felitsia Karpovna, who'd been standing alongside other uncles' wives on a long bench in the last row, to suddenly run forward—she somehow slapped a huge shako with a plume right over her bonnet, the shako having appeared out of nowhere, most likely prepared in advance for antics—and then gather her skirt up to her knee and imitate a daring hussar, twist an imaginary mustache on her finger, and place a foot on the settee, the same magnificent settee where The Immortal One himself sat enthroned amongst silk waterfalls and velvet pagodas constructed of small pillows.

They were treating him at the time with a sense of especially trembling deference admixed with joyous surprise and wary curiosity, since it was very recently, on St. Spiridon's Feast Day (meaning only a few days before this Christmas photo), that The Immortal One had inadvertently turned up in the storage room, where he'd been lying for many years under a heap of basins and battle canvases panegyrizing the exploits of omnifarious swordsmen.

Uncle Seraphim unearthed him. And that might not have happened if not for Uncle Pavel's fib. It was Uncle Pavel who instilled in Seraphim the idea that somewhere in the south of Malach's house (a place Uncle Pavel had once gone, propelled by a passion for all manner of adventure) there existed a wonderful room with vaulted ceilings and lusciously glistening stained glass in high, arch-shaped windows, and that within that room, which was gloriously illuminated from morning to night by varying colorful rays of light, one could apparently hear voices—one could hear, in some peculiar way, conversations between Semyon and Annushka, and Malach and many of the uncles, all intoned by them some time long ago, but not in that room at all, "not in the south, Fima, but in the north of the house, I swear to the Holy Mother!"

And so, Uncle Seraphim, suffused with an insatiable inquisitiveness, set off in search of that room. On the eve of his departure, he frightened everyone with his detached appearance, though it might more accurately be called an essentially dreamy and menacing concentration that caught hold of him ever more frequently and ever more strongly as the years passed, becoming more and more unfounded and ill-defined until, one day, alas, it was discovered that obviously the wisest of the uncles had, to the amusement and joy of the mocking sons-in-law, irrevocably submerged his entire being into that invincible concentration, transforming himself, as Annushka bitterly said, into "a brainless Petrushka." Armed with a hefty loupe, he made a long, thorough study of the uncommonly detailed, colorful, and obviously fantastical map of the southern outskirts of the house Uncle Pavel had compiled. Apart from the sideboards, cabinets, bureaus, console tables, étagères, mirrors, floor clocks, ottomans, and all manner of divans; apart from the flights of stairs, stoves, endless enfilades, columns, galleries and little, dead-end rooms, and innumerable corridors, there were some things absolutely inconceivable marked on the map: lakes in giant halls with half-dilapidated pilasters, collapsed walls and deep niches completely filled with shrubbery, sands covering huge expanses that had long ago swallowed up various furniture, thickets of reeds along rotted runner rugs, and boulders that had come out of nowhere, insidious "ghost doors" that seemed to disappear as soon as a wayfarer approached, habitats for kite birds and monitor lizards, and even kurgan stelae, God only knew how they'd ended up on the windowsills and cabinets …

It's not known if Uncle Seraphim saw all that.

It was told that he headed south early in the morning but quickly strayed from his path. Toward midday he checked his location against Uncle Pavel's map and discovered, to his considerable chagrin, that he was somewhere in the southeast and, moreover, extremely far from the enigmatic room marked on the map with an inordinately bold cross. After pondering this, Uncle Seraphim decided to turn back.

He walked a long time toward the northwest, through long corridors, spacious halls, dazzlingly bright galleries, and hopelessly dreary enfilades; he opened one high door with copper handles after another; crossed from room to room as cautiously and quietly as a ghost; examined along the way girandoles of "exceptional beauty" on peeling walls; but only toward evening did he surmise he was walking in a circle.

And it was then that he pushed—flung open, so it was said, in an outburst of desperation (or was it a fit of furious curiosity?)—a timeworn little door on rusty hinges, all eaten away by beetles, the very same little door (oh, holiday of circumstance!) behind which Malach's storage room was located, enticingly hidden in a narrow niche within a mossy old corner of an unprepossessing hall.

Using a kerosene lamp to light the storage room, Uncle Seraphim suddenly saw the woolen cloak with field epaulettes that Malach had worn during the times he'd wandered the unheated southern rooms on winter evenings; he then saw Malach's hat, a *papakha* of iridescent Teheran lambskin, in the humble company of foul rags, and then, a bit later, as he sorted through cracked paintings, most of them adorned with invincible, fantastically puffy-mustached and bulky-haunched horsemen who were annihilating foot soldiers with opulent broadswords, some impetuously and happily, some with gloomy ferocity, and some with mischievous grace, he stumbled upon Malach himself.

The Immortal One was sleeping a slumber that was persistent and deep, but (so it seemed to Uncle Seraphim) far from oblivious. Malach would frown, either alarmed by something or agonizingly vexed, then marvel at something in fright. Fleeting but apparently distinct dreams rushed before him in an endless series, leaving no gap for either a sudden awakening or a slow incursion of majestic emptiness. Those dreams persistently involved Malach in deceitfully significant and slyly confusing events; they held him in a narrow, rapidly moving stream, menacingly squeezed by powerful riverbanks that were the domains of reality and death, and that gave their word there would be a happy outcome; and they promised, perhaps generously, to fill his whole being—somewhere there, beyond that new curve—with an inexpressible bliss fit only for spirited dreams and impossible to experience on either of the two riverbanks. By all accounts, though, it was obvious that something irksome and bleak was arising in those fickle dreams, something far more decisive than the short-lived, unsteady, and mysteriously glorious thing that forced the feeble dreamer of dreams to shudder in that first moment and then brought about a rapturous smile that unexpectedly illuminated Malach's face, which was completely covered in sickly, shaggy hair; and then the smile disappeared without a trace as if it were a nimble fish, flashing like ghostly silver in the dark waters of a drowsy little lake ...

Only toward morning did Uncle Seraphim manage to awaken The Immortal One. Malach didn't recognize him. It almost seemed he wasn't even trying to recall the uncle, though he scrutinized him with a glum, unfriendly intentness, angrily moving a brow that an enterprising little spider studied with impunity. He seemed to want to frighten, or at least bewilder Seraphim with that hostile gaze. For his part, Seraphim looked upon his awakened parent with a cheery, exaggeratedly genial cordiality, "evincing not the slightest confusion," as he later told Annushka, even after a gloomy anxiety had seized Malach so strongly he had ("Can you believe it, Mamasha!") commenced snarling, oh, fierce demons! ... Malach commenced snarling at Uncle Seraphim, but Uncle Seraphim was not exactly completely calm: he was feeling uneasy in his own way—very uneasy in fact—but he was in that particular state where no force—even if it contained all the ferocity and all the fury of Hell—could deprive him of his equilibrium, which was all the more reason no snarling could possibly horrify, alarm, or even cause light discomfiture. In short, Uncle Seraphim had already been struck by a fit of splendid imperturbability. With the hope that his parent was on the verge of perceiving something familiar in his appearance, Seraphim bashfully and affectionately squinted as he raised his little spectacles (so narrow, they, too, seemed to be squinting) onto his forehead then saddled his reddened nose with them again, quickly ruffled his hair, tugged on his thin mustache, animatedly spun around, and showed himself this way and that ... but he didn't disappear anywhere, didn't dissolve, and didn't change, which by all appearances made The Immortal One uneasy: the images of reality that had suddenly eclipsed the fantastical world of Malach's flowing visions struck him unpleasantly for some time because of their insolent steadiness and artless clarity.

In the house, however, they explained otherwise the circumstances of Malach's thoroughly sullen dismay after the exceptionally proud Uncle Seraphim carried him to the hexagonal hall shortly before Christmas. They said the flighty daughters-in-law and their ever-insufficiently sober brothers-in-law (whose ruddy faces that day never parted from their monocles or from expressions of impassioned expedience), their sisters' mortally irksome sons-in-law, female cousins of the sisters' sons-in-law, husbands and sisters-in-law of those female cousins, and all manner of other relatives, many of whom, according to Annushka's accurate observation, The Immortal One had never even seen, because they hadn't appeared in the uncles' lives until after he'd happened to fall upon that triply cursed storage room, where he'd slept for ... Oh, righteous God! Nobody knows now how many years it was ... and so, thanks to the uncles' lack of supervision, all those unfortunate fools of daughters-in-law, their horribly unceremonious brothers-in-law, and the blockheaded sons-in-law created an overly spirited crush around the ottoman that stood, very stately, between the two wall mirrors where Seraphim had seated The Immortal One: everyone contrived—with far too much surprise, insistence, and inquisitiveness—to examine and even, on the sly, touch Malach, throwing him into a state of confusion.

That was the general opinion, an opinion shared by all but Uncle Semyon.

He contended that Malach had irrevocably lost his memory, and, perhaps, along with his memory, had also been deprived of his God-given ability to distinguish slumber from wakefulness, day from night, year from moment, and flesh from ethereality. He said everything was mixed up; everything was upended and muddled in the idol's senile brains. And it would be good if that chaos didn't turn to madness, dismal madness.

"O-o-oh, but hold on a moment, my dear brothers!" he said, sympathetically scaring them and taking pleasure as he noticed how his new intonation put them on their guard: it was gently caustic and completely uncharacteristic of his sort of prophesies. "Your precious little papa won't just snarl! . . . He'll bite the lot of you all over! He'll prowl around the house like a malicious apparition! And he'll ferociously set upon anyone he lays eyes on! Oh, but he will! . . ."

Of course, none of that happened, though a welcoming, idly contemplative serenity did not come to reign Malach's soul as quickly as many of the uncles expected. In any case, The Immortal One doesn't appear pacified in the Christmas photo in which Felitsia Karpovna imitates a hussar. Malach is looking at someone with the very same angry bewilderment as when he looked at Uncle Seraphim in the storage room; but who is it? Jacques, perhaps, who's just cried, "All set!" Or maybe Claude, who'd added, "Watch for zee mageecal bird!"

Only a few months later, toward the beginning of Holy Week, did Malach, as Annushka put it, "perk up in his heart." Meaning he remained as immobile as before, sitting, as before, for entire days at a time on the plump, rep-covered ottoman (he'd taken a liking to it back at Christmas), holding up his chin with a walking stick, and, as before, not recognizing any of the uncles, no matter what heartfelt speeches they addressed to their parent when they took turns sitting down with him. His ability to cast eyes upon everything and everyone with a cheerful, affectionate indifference had returned, though. And, as the luminoscribe's work documents, that happy ability hadn't left him at Easter, either, when Kikiani arrived to take photos after a telephone call from Annushka ("Ah, my dear Vikentii Samsonovich, I don't want to hear anything about those French buffoons any longer!"), nor had that ability left him by a later date, when Glaphira, Uncle Anastasy's third wife, was buried and, for some reason that was never determined—some said it was at the insistence of Annushka, who'd squabbled with Kikiani the previous day, though others insisted it was at the request of the widower himself, an indefatigable sinner who had long been passionately in love with the derisive Felitsia, who adored Jacques and Claude, calling them "darling Cavaliers-Chevaliers," and who seemed to have inclined that scatterbrained, aging ladies' man toward his blasphemous decision—photographing the funeral ceremony was entrusted to these jolly fellows and fops.

After miraculously escaping Annushka's disfavor, those very same shallow-minded Frenchmen took photographs a year later, too, the day of Uncle Anastasy's engagement to Josya's stepdaughter Polina, Felitsia Karpovna's eldest daughter. But The Immortal One isn't in those shots, which are immaculately sharp and imbued with a cold, impenetrable clarity (the artists did, after all, occasionally betray their lively, slovenly muse, who was but a simple, hurrying girl), shots in which, alas, one can't guess what motion preceded or followed any shot; in which Uncle Josya seems constrained by the air itself and, like everyone else in those dryly glossy photographs, pressed by some dense, ivory-colored expanse as he looks with sad reproach at Uncle Anastasy busily kissing, without any enjoyment whatsoever but also without any visible aversion ... ah, no, most likely he's examining—as if he weren't a groom but a dispassionately obliging and weak-sighted doctor—the gangly Polina's limp hand, remembering, perhaps, how, the day before yesterday, in the evening at Feoktist Prisiagin's bakery (where, by the way, Uncle Porphiry had also taken a fancy to holding noisy Sunday boozing sessions, even threatening more than once, on an unsober head, to set fire to that "devilishly wonderful establishment," due to excessive love), he'd so enjoyed kissing another hand, one alluringly small, and resilient, and willful, the very same little hand wearing heavy rings over lacy gloves (it was said Felitsia adored lace no less than she loved Jacques and Claude) that was now holding a pear-shaped goblet whose damp glass distorted the statuette of a shaggy Pan and the dial of the mantelpiece clock ... which read a quarter to six in the afternoon ...

Malach wasn't at Uncle Anastasy's wedding, either. After sitting for more than a year on the ottoman, with which it seemed he'd never part, The Immortal One stood one morning, surprising everyone with his decisive, combative, and lively appearance, and spryly exited the hexagonal hall through the south door, humming "The Hunter's March," whose buoyantly ill-tempered sounds, "tum-pa-ba-bim! bim-pa-ba-bam!" may have enlivened him after unexpectedly returning to him during his half-doze. None of the uncles doubted their willful parent—who'd suddenly livened up, not only in his heart, but also in his ancient body, which was as light as air, having withered and become freed of restlessly circulating vital fluids—was making his way ("May Satan swallow him out there!" Annushka burst out in a fit of pique) back to the little storage room. However, none of them—neither Uncle Seraphim, who set out aiming to block his parent's passage and had even spread his arms in the doorway, but then backed right off; nor Uncle Pavel, who promised Annushka a minute later that he would catch right up with dear Papa, seize him, carry him back, and sit him on the ottoman; nor Uncle Nestor, who'd offered to lend a hand to his brother in any way, "if, of course, you need it, Pavlusha"—dared stop Malach; because, in the first place it was clear to everyone that it wasn't whim or empty fancy, as Annushka thought, but a commanding, vindictive, and invincible power that drew Malach to the distant storage room, which held him, perhaps captivated by the infallible pitch-black gloominess that deceptively resembled an unattainable death; and because, in the second place, their parent's face could have frightened any of the uncles that morning. For on that morning Malach Grigorevich looked just as fervid, irreconcilably menacing, and ruthlessly happy as an unknown luminoscribe had once captured him somewhere on the southwestern front in Galicia, near a heap of wheels, bent frames, and hacked-up bodies (all that remained of the incautious Austro-Hungarian bicycle squadron that had entered into battle with the Cossack mounted patrol), and just the same as he'd appeared to Annushka a little later in the horrifying dream that prompted her to quickly fulfill Antipatros's final behest of turning the little baby in at the damned orphanage, tearing and seizing that live, warm treasure from her heart because the monster's cold head with the gaping mouth hadn't been torn off and hadn't fallen into the tall grass! ... Because the monster was already returning from the war in full health, armed with a pike, a rifle, and a devilishly sharp saber! Because it was already making its way home, maybe from the west, maybe from the east! Because it was already wending through colorful Sarmatian or reddish Nogai plains, ferocious as it frightened hoopoes and lizards, heading toward those same tall front doors the inspired Greek had flung open to

Love on that crystalline, starry night! . . . Because, in the end, oh, light-haired bards and dark-skinned rishis, Uncle Semyon was not the sort of staid taleteller who would plink at the most cherished strings of his slighted soul, speaking without tears and dudgeon, and without pitiful gestures and sighs, about how, on another starless night, they'd brought him, good God!, to a sorry orphanage as if he were unneeded rags, in a tatty chest far more crowded and stuffy than the storage room reeking of rot that had turned into a gaol for the idol (oh, Heavenly Powers, Your vengeance for the baby's sufferings is modest).

The orphanage (ah, the poor uncle did, after all, need to calm down, he needed to, "if only, son, to illuminate for a moment the mournfully precious details with the light of a pacified heart!") was located in the dreary depths of a half-rotted wooden structure whose façade was overgrown by scraggly vines and insolent bindweed, and it stood in a sickly garden square surrounded by a low chain fence. Felitsia Karpovna hadn't, thank God, forgotten the Greek's generosity, so she waited in that same garden square—which abutted Trinity Square from the north and was uncomfortably dank, neglected, and crammed with cicadas and crickets, which drowned out the ingratiating burble of reeking, unseen waters—and lurked in the tall bushes near the orphanage's plank gates, watching for the one-handed junior officer Sashenka, the traitor Josya, and the *sotnik* Pavel.

As soon as they'd gotten out of the automobile, which they left with its headlights extinguished beside the fountain in the middle of an avenue lined with chestnut trees and paved with coquina limestone that ran from Troitsky Square, through the garden square, and to the orphanage, Felitsia ran to meet them, flapping a white hankie three times as Uncle Pavel had arranged with her by telephone ("if everything is as it should be, miss …"), and then led them into the orphanage's yard and a small building with one window, where a dreadfully unsober orphanage guard slept on the tiled stove, a saber at his waist. Felitsia announced with a sly smile that it was she who'd sent the guard some vicious mead for dinner, two *shtof* worth, nearly a fifth of a bucket, if expressed in vodka terms, which was allegedly from Prince Cherkesov in honor of the holiday for Saint Zosima, patron and protector of beekeepers. She thought the guard unlikely to awaken before dawn, and then at dawn—"You should leave the chest here, gentlemen!"—he would accidentally discover the baby and, of course, bring him to Felitsia Karpovna right away, guiltily blinking his eyes. And Felitsia Karpovna, my good men, would be tenderly surprised when she saw the sweet foundling and then rebuke the brainless reveling guard with a good tongue-lashing, because he— have mercy, my lady—hadn't managed, thanks to his disastrous in-sensitivity, to ascertain what miscreants had disposed of the little one or when, and because the baby might have languished all night in the gatehouse, bawling from hunger and sorrow.

"In short, everything will work out in the best possible way!" promised the bought-off matron with ardent affability.

That affability, however, didn't even begin to prevent Uncle Pavel—who'd attached, as he himself expressed it, "more hopes on a menacing word than on tempting gold"—from sternly assuring the matron that he would give her quite the peppering if she suddenly got it into her head to inform the most esteemed gentleman patron, who was closely acquainted with Malach, or anyone else whatsoever about the baby's provenance.

With that, all three showily took leave of their slightly vexed accomplice, who was secretly favorable to taking tea with the en-chanting mustachioed men; all three kissed the newfound orphan, bowing in turn over the opened chest ("Judas, son, smelled horribly of gasoline!"), and left without further delay, because dawn was al-ready nearing, darting off in the unforgettable Dux and lighting the deserted city streets with carbide headlights.

And so, according to legend ("legend thought up by Semyon Malachovich, of course," Felitsia Karpovna once swore to Annushka, thrice making the sign of the cross over herself), Antipatros's son landed in an orphanage … And on that same night, there collapsed in Malach's house a solid wall, behind which an unknown hall had been hiding, and these words appeared out of nowhere on the orphanage's plank gate:

Everyone is orphaned and wretched in this world.

PART IV
GOLDEN PINE

After some time had passed, yet another miracle occurred. It was late in the evening, the very same evening that Annushka stole a revolver from Uncle Pavel in a fit of restive offense at the ruthless fate that had separated her first from her beloved, then from her baby Syomushka: she had intended to fire a piercing bullet into her own small heart, which overflowed with sorrow, but then someone's wary hand very quietly knocked on a window of Malach's home. This was one of the many windows in Uncle Pavel's vast office: the fourteenth window if counted from a blind wall densely hung with sabers, pikes, and partizans, the eastern wall beside which Uncle Pavel soundly slept on a couch in his boots and uniform.

It was next to that window that the forlorn Annushka stood in a pose of sorrowful mettle, revolver at her breast and head thrown back—"Like this!" said Uncle Semyon, demonstrating—with the thousand-eyed Azrael's black wings already spread ("He'd already greedily extended them, son!") over her.

Annushka moved the drapes aside and flung open the window when she heard the knock. A lone horseman entered her sight: the long locks of his mountain *papakha* hid his face, and a rifle hung on his back. He was wearing a Cossack guard's long *chekmen* jacket with silver braid trim, and his long drawers of white serge, like those worn by the tumbling Abyssinian acrobats in the Greek's circus, shone like pearls in the fleeting moonlight.

Without saying a word, the horseman waited for the moment when Annushka, having scrutinized him, finally dropped the revolver (which had been inexplicably aimed at him), stupefied and bewildered. He cautiously placed a small envelope sealed with wax in her now-empty hand, immediately turned the impatiently prancing horse under him, then jumped over the front-garden fences, first the near fence, then the far fence, and quickly rushed away from Malach's home, into the pitch dark.

Annushka unsealed the envelope, pulled out a thin sheet of letter paper, and glancing at it in a flash of moonlight that had torn through a shaggy cloud, she gasped.

It was a letter from the Greek.

"Here it is!" Uncle Semyon cried out, pointing at his chest. "Here

it is! Here it is!" he repeated, shifting so he was under the chandelier. And only when he was already under the chandelier and his
entire body had suddenly buckled, as if someone had shoved snow
down the front of his shirt, did he slowly thrust his hand into the
inner pocket of his jacket and then, just as slowly, without changing
his pose or paying any heed to Annushka—who was observing him
with growing concern and even endeavoring to contradict him from
her corner, where the squeaking of the bentwood chair was intensifying and transforming into an uneasy music—he extracted and
brought to light Antipatros's heaven-sent missive that the mysterious
horseman in the mountain *papakha* had delivered to Annushka that
frightening night, forestalling the nimble angel of death …

After that scene, Uncle Semyon straightened to his full height,
sighed deeply, and then waved the precious little sheet of paper in the
air for a long time, smoothing it thoroughly on his palm, and wiggling
his brows, lips, cheeks, and all the other parts of his face, though he
began reading only once his face had frozen as if it had groped about
within itself for the proper expression—an expression of sadness and
inspiration's wings.

He read in a soft, slightly quivering, and agitatedly tender voice
that merged youth and courage, and drew elation and sorrow into
itself. He read as he had never before read any of his roles because—
can you imagine, Melpomene and Thalia!—he read without any pre-
meditated intonations and without any measured pauses, well-tuned
breaths, or prepared accents on the words, as if he were reading in
his very own voice. But this was the voice of his parent, this was the
voice of Antipatros himself, pouring out naturally and freely, right
from the uncle's heart:

"My incomparable Annushka! Oh, my life and fate!

"Do you remember the Hetman Garden, the crowns of chestnut
and linden trees illuminated by flashes of fancy fireworks, the lights
of carousels and traveling shows, and the sounds of a fleeting *uhlan*
mazurka, which carried into the spring dusk from a high stage
adorned with colorful flags? Do you remember how the sedate fire
captain lovingly conducted a harmonious orchestra, conveying greet-
ings to the ladies over his shoulder, and how the quiet steppe stars

furtively began blazing over the garden and, soon after, in the wide windows of the hetman's boxy palace … Barely had darkness fallen when your ardent Greek, your dark-skinned magician aflame with passion, rushed headlong in his silent chariot along a wondrous avenue and through light arches, toward the meeting place you'd set for him, a treasured rotunda wound in vines. And it was there, during those exhilarating moments after the weary orchestra had gone silent, after the timpani had been given free rein in parting, and a fiery-mustachioed court bugler in galloons had stood stock-still on the granite steps of the portal, completely surrounded by sparkly radiance after performing 'The Changing of the Guard' three times, that you said, 'Oh, Antipatros! Oh, my sorcerer! The night is short: Dawn will spirit away the constellations in the heavens but the constellations of your kisses will burn brighter in my heart, my love, than the heavenly constellations!' Oh, Annushka! …"

That is what the Greek wrote in Greek.

In Russian, the Greek wrote to Annushka that he regretted not having properly explained to her (depending, as he was, on the feminine guile within her heart) at their moment of leave-taking before his hasty departure to Africa, exactly how she should wind the old dimwit around her finger when he returned from the war. And he would return very soon. "Your Malach, precious Annushka, my one and only, will return from the war any day now, and your dream will come true any day now, too," he assured her. And he was assuring for a real reason. It was not only Annushka's dream, which the Greek miraculously knew about, that foretold The Immortal One's imminent return. Verity itself foretold his return: that battles in various places around the planet were losing, little by little, their bygone grandeur and, in certain places, were completely wrapping up or taking on the very same unhappy, gloomy, wait-and-see character that Uncle Izmail's confrontation with the insidious legions of mysterious insects was fated to acquire in the days when Porphiry's estate grew wild; and that Emperor Franz Joseph, who on sleepless nights had simple-minded visions of flogging King Peter I Kara! or! evi" in Schönbrunn with some very nice switches indeed ("Single-handedly and accompanied by an orchestra!" his wicked demons encouraged), already happened to have passed away; and that Emperor Wilhelm Hohenzollern was already unable to explain with any befittingly lofty inspiration, to either his irritated allies or surprised enemies, behind what cunning devil or under whose artistic command his naval destroyers were swarming the Java Sea, covering its lightly gleaming waters with puzzling patterns and maliciously bombarding the capes of Kalimantan; and that the San Marino captain regents, always distinguished by their foresight, had already ordered all soldiers of the Most Serene Republic, which, as was sincerely stated in the order, "was exuberantly convinced of its heroic lack of importance," to quickly return to the tiny motherland after handing over to any of the Entente states an aeroplane that had remained miraculously intact so it could be used in further flights and heroics within the boundless expanse of battle; and that an out-of-favor kaiseresque mustache had appeared once again, as if nothing had happened, having disappeared the day Archduke Ferdinand was buried, disappearing right out from under a powerful Swabian nose sensitive to the winds of "world politics"—that nose sat on the face of luminoscribe Friedrich Zoiter, whose fabulous work (Annushka in luxurious sultan's garb among guards with *yataghans*, fan-waving servants, and peacocks … the lone gusli player, Malach, on the edge of a magnificent oak forest) had been familiar to all the uncles since childhood; and that several enlightened Himalayan kingdoms had followed the Most Serene Republic and were already elevating their own insignificance to valor, too, enabling them to display their disregard for the great struggle of nations that was continuing—Uncle Pavel, at any rate, with his passion for cloak-and-dagger aeronautics, was still enthusiastically sketching out abstruse diagrams on a huge map of Central Africa, contemplating certain secret flights ("Why? What's the reason, Pavlusha?" asked an astonished and frightened Annushka) over the Gulf of Guinea and the Cameroonian volcanoes, and Uncle Alexander still constructed and blew up viaducts in the insidiously chasmy mountains of Kurdistan, and Uncle Nestor, who'd recovered from his wound, from the tricky wound that had generated that peculiar and eternal tilt of his head, like a performing violinist's, was still hollering out a threatening "Fire!" in Transylvania and sending shell fougasses into Austro-Hungarian troops' trenches and reinforcements ...

"But," wrote the Greek, "no matter what characteristics this verity from around the world now evinces, Annushka must pluck up her courage on those uneasy days, despite the circumstances. This means Annushka should not comfort herself, out of fear, with the dangerous fantasy that her Malach Grigorevich is still far from home, that he's just slowly flying along somewhere over duned El Hamada in a decorated hot-air balloon, heading in the direction of the Black Sea through the windless air of Arabian skies devastated by a furious sun, or somehow riding toward sunrise in a rattling, crumpled Russo-Balt automobile on a remote road through Podolia teeming with thieves and deserters, or barely making any progress at all, moving sinfully slowly toward sunset in a crowded, squeaky wagon drawn by sleepy harnessed yaks along rutted mountain paths of the sky-high realm of Druk Yul in the sparsely populated kingdom of Bhutan, so blissfully lost in the Himalayas ... Oh no, Annushka should instead dream about the same thing she dreamt about this evening as she pressed the revolver's cold barrel—Oh, God!—to her heart ... Let her contemplate, as she contemplated a moment ago, that Malach is already very close now, that he's already wandering somewhere in the house's southern halls in a torn cloak, searching for a favorable route north to Annushka's cozy bedroom—and he's already destroying moldering étagères and rusted-out tins with a gleaming saber, straying through western corridors that are distinguished, according to Pavel Malachovich's information, by a maliciously intricate floor plan and monstrous clutter—and he's already using a heavy spear to break down the secret, low eastern door that looks onto the Nogai steppes and will be overgrown with mighty, wild grass by fall. And let her! ... But that's not at all why she should create those pictures for herself: not for a bullet to end up in her heart, but for her to summon the determination to meet Malach at any moment, so Malach wouldn't catch her unawares, no matter how deviously and suddenly he might turn up.

She needed to greet him with a smile—serenely, welcomingly, and even affectionately—as if there were not and had never been any Greek she'd loved so madly, as if there were not and had never been any baby Syomushka from whom fate had parted her. And if precious Annushka could greet Malach the way the Greek was now teaching her, then her heart would be ready for the sublime deceit that lay ahead of her, and that she would carry out in order to save Syomushka! ...

After some time had passed, she should tell Malach this: a vision had come to her. And that vision was frightful, just frightful! Dead people had come to her in her sleep. Great numbers of them. And they were all wearing epaulettes, uniforms, and outlandish medals and ribbons. And they were all spinning, jumping, and dancing, though they didn't all have arms and legs. And only one among them didn't dance. He was tall. And he was dressed in civilian clothes, a black frock coat. But he stood, soldier-like, almost at attention. And held his head soldier-like. He held his head proudly and sternly in his bent left arm, as if it were a uniform's peaked cap. When Annushka asked why he wasn't dancing like the others, he whispered to her, with the lips of the head that sat on his palm and that he put close to Annushka's ear, that only the earthly warriors Malach had hacked to pieces during the war were dancing. And he was no earthly warrior. He was a heavenly warrior. He was a guardian angel, assigned to Malach by Heaven's will. "That's who I am now," the angel suddenly burst out. "Because your Malach chopped those valorous warriors too maliciously, brandished his saber too savagely in war. And one day ... this was in Galicia, on the bank of a small, smelly brook, a brook called Golden Pine ... Malach was riding along the river bank on a horse. He was riding unhurriedly, at an easy trot, effortlessly catching up to an army bicycle that wobbled from side to side, ridden by an Austrian soldier trying to save himself from Malach's saber: he was a young mechanic from the unfortunate and audacious bicycle company that had courageously wheeled out of the riverside forest on their fragile, rattling machines and hurried along the slope of the hill to attack a mounted Cossack detachment, and whose jubilation matched the character of that May day—the sun was shining so much and reflecting so much off the skinny commander's round glasses! ... The company mechanic—do you hear me, Annushka?—

was the only one left in one piece after that brisk attack. But Malach had already caught up. Malach was already at his back. And I was at Malach's back. And when Malach waved his saber with unpremeditated ferocity, bringing it far, far behind his back to hack off the Austrian bicycle mechanic's unprotected, youthful head in one blow, he hacked off the head of his guardian angel along with that small shorn head. Both heads—one visibly, the other invisibly—rolled into Golden Pine Brook. And at that very same hour, on another river, on a river called Mürz, in the city of Mürzzuschlag, the soft, damp head of a baby protruded from a woman's womb: the baby was already half-orphaned because that baby was the son of the bicycle mechanic whose head the murky vernal waters of Golden Pine Brook hid from the light. The baby's mother, the wife of the bicycle mechanic, passed away during childbirth … And so, sweet Annushka, take my head and give it to Malach as a memento of the battle on the Golden Pine!" the Angel told her. He told her and vanished. And Annushka woke up. But Annushka managed to hear a voice just at the moment she awoke, while the mysterious power of the vision still lingered, competing with the morning's real sounds and images. And that edifyingly affectionate and welcomingly commanding voice uttered these words, "Annushka, do not accept the angel's head! It will return to its place—to the shoulders of the heavenly warrior guarding your husband's soul—by itself. But that will only happen when you and Malach Grigorevich bring a baby into your home from the orphanage on Troitsky Square, some unfortunate orphan who's just as lonely and fine as the one who was born in the city of Mürzzuschlag at that wicked hour!…"

The Greek instructed Annushka to tell Malach all that. After telling Malach, she should begin imploring him to do what the voice ordered. Of course, Malach would object. He would say it didn't concern him whose heads were coming into the world from female wombs and whose were hidden in a river's dark waters at the time he was at war on the southwestern front. He would say that at war there are no living and dead, there is no rage and mercy, there is no bravery and cowardice: at war there is only war. Malach, after all, was born for war. A warrior. And only war preserves his soul, only war instills in his soul a bright and stable serenity, because Malach is in his element at war. And his purpose is to fight without experiencing either love or contempt for the vanquished: the absence of those emotions in the warrior's heart is called valor. Valor rules Malach's heart, which is illuminated by valor. And valor does not allow Malach to reconsider the sorrowful or fortunate fates of every possible soldier and baby. As for the guardian angel who had come to Annushka, Malach doesn't much care if he has a head or doesn't have a head. That's what Malach would tell her.

But Annushka should hold her own, sob, and beseech Malach to spare her soul, telling him the horrifying vision had begun coming round to see her every night. That it gets more and more dreadful each time! That the beheaded angel had already broken into dance! That Annushka had already seen Malach himself amongst the dancers. And that he possessed two heads: one being his own, the other being the angel's, the head the angel had given him! …

"And so, my precious Annushka, when Malach yields to your pleas and tears, raising heart above valor—for tenderness is above valor, as you know!—when he arrives at the orphanage with you, agreeing to accommodate the unknown force tormenting your soul with weighty visions and adopt an orphaned baby chosen at random, the matron Felitsia will take matters in hand.

"She will begin showing you various babies and tell you a bit about each. Our Syomushka will be among them, and she will contrive this story about him: he was found one morning on the doorstep of the orphanage's guard hut, all trembling from cold because he was wrapped up, the poor wretch, in only one thin swaddling cloth on which there was embroidered a little golden pine tree, in golden thread …

"'Ah!' you'll call out, interrupting Felitsia, 'That's it, that's our sign, Malach Grigorevich … Golden Pine!'

"Remember that, Annushka: Golden Pine. Tree and river. Adieu.

"Adieu, my unforgettable Annushka, wife of the *yesaul*! Eternally bearing the radiant wound of love in my heart, I am

"Your Antipatros"

PART V
TIMES

Malach's return from the war was such that nobody in the house knew how or when it had happened.

By all appearances, they said, he'd returned long before Uncle Seraphim noticed him deep within the Caucasian enfilade, within a walk-through, tapering expanse of completely deserted rooms that stretched in the direction of the Caucasus, rooms that were, for some long-forgotten reason, considered impenetrable ("And what do you know, Mamasha, he showed up in distant doorways but disappeared just like that!"); long before Uncle Pavel announced he'd certainly seen his parent in one of the pantries ("the one furthest south, Mamasha, you've never been there") among a crowd of spongers zealously dividing up liqueurs amongst themselves, but then, alas, lost sight of him; and it was even before Uncle Alexander had either imagined something because of all his sleepless reeling around the house, caused by fear of the drowned woman who was taking nightly revenge upon him on behalf of his intrepid sons, the pontoniers he'd rashly led to their deaths in that unknown tributary of the distant Tigris; or perhaps he truly had crossed paths with a certain very nimble figure "who resembled Papenka in some way" in the circular corridor edging the billiard room.

It was said that all those visions and observations were preceded by an announcement from Yelizar, the steward, who had established some time ago—on his own initiative and while feeling the effects of an inspiring evening-time lack of sobriety, as if to atone for his continuous drunkenness—the practice of making inordinately verbose and extraordinarily rational reports to Annushka regarding household matters, reports which, it must be said, agonized her no less than his penitential morning speeches performed with a hung-over, tied tongue.

One day the steward came to Annushka with a report that informed her, among other things, that a skinny-legged, little palomino horse with a cavalry saddle had been wandering somewhere in the house's eastern halls for who knew how many days, inflicting noticeable damage to the parquet; the steward had already appealed to Pavel Malachovich (whose disastrous habit of neglecting the horse tethers their parent had installed around the front entrance may also have been familiar to his mother, the *yesaul's* wife), asking if perhaps it was his horse that had mounted the steps, headed into the house, and lost its way. But the enraged Pavel Malachovich answered that his horse was a light chestnut color and didn't suffer whatsoever from skinny-leggedness—quite the contrary, it had strong legs and a very deep chest—leaving the steward to ponder whether he should send the stray little horse off the premises the next day by capturing it with the coachman's assistance, though he wondered if the missus, the *yesaul's* wife, might then announce in advance her own instructions regarding the possible capture, which, if approached irrationally, would generate considerable havoc and noise in the eastern halls.

In the beginning, it never even occurred to Annushka that Malach might have ridden home on the mysterious horse that had gotten into the house by unknown means, which was all the more reason she didn't announce any instructions to the steward Yelizar, since dispatches of this sort, which inevitably reached her heart, a place indifferent to intricate particulars, were invariably classified there under the generic and distressing caption, *Regarding Household Troubles of Any Kind,* and provoked the very same complex feeling of indignant hurt pride, perplexity, and guilt (a feeling pernicious to the lively spirit of household management) she experienced when she listened to Uncle Pavel's stories about the horrifying dust storms that apparently struck the southwest of the house during the second half of May, which had taken on such an infernal strength that by St. Feodosia's Day there was not only dust hurtling through some of the passageways ("Can you imagine, Mamenka!"), but airy étagères and even entire massive chests of drawers were bouncing and rolling around like dried baby's breath. His stories of something even more frightening, albeit not as fierce, had the same effect: Uncle Pavel suggested to her that the lounging spongers scattered around the distant halls and rooms were present in completely unimaginable, completely devilish, abundance.

"Oh and you generated at least a thousand of them! ... At least! At least, dear heart!" he would insist, not yielding a bit to Annushka, who would answer him, taking offense, that spongers can't just gather in such abominable quantities in decent homes, and that if she'd needed, for the sake of Christ, to shelter dozens of, or even, fine, one dozen, pathetics (she simply said *pathetics*, and here her favorite adjective slyly did not respond to the question "what kind of people?" deigning instead to answer only the question "who?" and masquerade as the part of speech that carries an imprint of a certain divine detachment, without touching on Annushka's attitude toward those very peculiar *pathetics*, toward the pathetic and majestic, portly and frail, haughty and meek, slovenly and tidy, submissive and flighty, hilariously varied, and, in their own way, picturesque creatures for whom she nurtured an obvious weakness), and so if she happened to harbor a dozen or two of them, that didn't mean at all that she was a guilty party to all the abominable behavior taking place within the house; and, even more so, she wasn't a party to all the *particular* abominable behavior noticed exclusively by Uncle Pavel, who may have had occasion to meet startling quantities of spongers of numerous varieties while strolling around Malach's home … it was true. But as for her, she said, now with dreamy regret rather than offense, only Lavr Selantevich ever seemed to catch her eye, and this "Syomushka's Lavrusha," as she'd subsequently begun to refer to that pathetic, had, in her stern opinion (which of course expressed a condescending jealousy of a particular type) "become too much of a bosom friend" to Uncle Semyon.

And Lavr Selantevich truly was the only one in the house Uncle Semyon permitted to cross the threshold of his office at those special hours when only the daughters of Zeus and Mnemosyne were allowed ("They descended, son, from Helicon's blissful heights on glistening wings!"), meaning when Uncle Semyon was dressed in his baggy, burgundy robe with sheets of paper in his hand, learning a new role in front of a cheval mirror, addressing words—self-willed and not yet caught in the snares of his inspiration—to either the floor clock in the corner or his double in the clouded silver depths of the dilapidated glass. Sometimes Uncle Semyon himself even flung open the door of his office when he heard Lavrusha's voice nearby and proclaimed, "You're here, Lavr, you wretched old man! You're here, you weed of my soul! So then, why aren't you hurrying to ascend to my chambers, you miserable person? Or do you hazard to pay for my benevolence with arrogance? I will reduce it to disfavor in a single instant, as you know!"

To which Lavr Selantevich replied without delay from the neighboring halls, "I've yet to poison the wild demonic choir in my heart, with sloe liqueur; but new misfortune clouds my heart for your harsh reproach is born of ire ..."

But Uncle Semyon did not hear his wordy and interminable (this was only the curtain-raiser) answer. That venomously triumphant intonation he'd vainly been attempting to find by "sampling," as he expressed it, or "taking a bite" of monologues and cues from the new play suddenly emerged all by itself in those words he addressed to Lavrusha, and then Uncle Semyon quickly, but also carefully, tiptoed, as if he were afraid of spilling the unexpectedly acquired intonation during his dash into the depths of his office, to the mirror. Meanwhile, Lavr Selantevich remained in place, explaining with growing animation why he hadn't hurried—to this day he hadn't hurried—to come to Uncle Semyon ... Oh! Because, as it turned out, the malicious-tongued demons who'd settled in his heart were not as sensitive to sloe liqueur as to light-colored, bitter orange liqueur, so now he was poisoning them with light-colored bitter orange; and because the thrice-cursed gout had tormented him, "more dreadful than which are only those pearls of your wrath; you, proud ward of Helicon's girls"; and because Annushka had hidden the anise vodka that would have instantaneously saved Lavr Selantevich from both demons and gout, and perhaps even given him wings, on which he would have flown off to Uncle Semyon ...

"You'll make it the rest of the way on foot," Annushka told him.

It should be stated that she'd been displaying an overly noticeable unfriendliness toward Lavr Selantevich ever since she'd taken it into her head that it was he, Lavrusha, an old-fashioned tragic actor with a regal bass, who'd decorously tippled away his whole life in the pantry and always spoke in verse ("about all sorts of trifles!" she sighed), who'd instilled in Syomushka a passion for acting. At times she even insisted Lavrusha had shown up at the house after he'd become a pathetic, at the very same time, as bad luck would have it, that Uncle Semyon had just learned to walk and was thirstily soaking up every image and every sound with his exultant infantile mind.

"And that," she argued, "was when Lavrusha latched onto Syomushka's delicate intellect, like a burr on a velvet ribbon."

Others among the uncles attempted in vain to object, saying Lavrusha certainly could have latched onto Nikita Malachovich's infant mind the same way, while he was at it, and Mokei Malachovich's, too, since he'd been born right on Nikita's heels, or to any other uncle, even the very eldest. And it was pointless for Uncle Pavel to show her a photograph, a luminous work by Friedrich Zoiter in which fuzzy-fleeced sheep and broad-hipped goats graze in a cozy gorge under the mighty crowns of stubby elm trees; where the currents of glistening waterfalls hurl themselves over rocks right and left; where slender-legged naiad maidens blissfully dance, treading along a lake; where shaggy fauns in willow crowns lay themselves on branches of an unembraceable oak; where a satisfied horse-tailed satyr takes flight after leaping over a shaggy tamarisk bush with his head thrown back, having caught an incautious wood nymph in a nearby beech grove; and where, finally, Lavrusha is sitting on a plaster boulder, picturesquely got up in an animal hide and depicting Pan, and Annushka's firstborn is a shepherd who plays on the reed pipe for Pan, whence, of course, it follows that Lavrusha knew Uncle Porphiry in his adolescent days, too, and that, hence, this pathetic had been sponging since times unknowable, since the times Annushka herself called *Zoiter times.*

The power of Annushka's memory, however—or perhaps more aptly stated, its exultant weakness—enabled her to connect any time endowed with its own spirit and nature to the eternal Zoiter times, when Malach and Annushka, their eldest son, and the sponger Lavrusha, too, as well as, of course, the luminoscribe Zoiter himself, were all born. Even the time when the great struggle between nations was waning, when poor Uncle Semyon dwelled at the orphanage under the watch of the deceitful and sinning Felitsia, a time remembered by many of its denizens (the elder uncles in any case) as disturbing and alarming, and a time differentiated by its distinctive and inordinate fluidity, no, even that time did not uncover the slightest attributes of painful detachment within Annushka's fading memory, where it bordered on the immovable, immense, and bottomless Zoiter times that were as dear to Annushka's heart as the luminoscribe Zoiter himself. Zoiter, who perennially takes photographs with a Ludwig Moser stereoscopic camera in the depths of those magical times that spread in all directions; rather like the inextinguishable light that comes from a sun lost in infinity—and also comes from a tiny studio with a glass-domed ceiling on the corner of Peschanaya and Komitetskaya streets, where the inspired Zoiter obeys his finicky muse by continuously changing landscapes and panoramas drawn on screens and panels made of albumen paper, but where nothing else changes.

And yet the time under discussion here, despite the traits it might have possessed—irrepressible fluidity, tempestuous impetuosity, or a spellbinding serene stillness akin to what suddenly settled in the minute before shooting a photograph, and which presaged a fit of ferocious inspiration in the luminoscribe Zoiter's clear eyes—ought, for the sake of truthfulness, be called the time of Uncle Semyon's confinement in the orphanage, or perhaps simply *orphan time*, as Uncle Semyon called it, deeming that the only relationship Zoiter times had to orphan time was that Friedrich Karlovich Zoiter, who hadn't taken photos for a long time (the Society of Mutual Credits had been awarded his photography studio as payment of debts even before the Russo-Japanese war, then boastfully founded an orangery there, which soon burned to the ground), frequently visited Annushka during them, treating her to conversations about this and that, mostly about the state of affairs "in dee global theater of military action," and transforming little by little into a pathetic under the effect of Annushka's benevolence and under the influence of his old friend Lavrusha, who first trained him in the ways of the pantry, gave him a taste for strong liqueurs and vodka, and then showed him certain expanses in the southeast of Malach's house ("barely habitable, son, but very restful"), where Friedrich Karlovich gradually settled in and where, as a matter of fact, according to Uncle Pavel's assurances, "only Germans" had ever resided.

And it befell Zoiter—roughly a month and a half after Annushka told him about the steward's surprising observation—to clearly recollect that the exact same type of horse Yelizar Afanasevich described to her in his report had been given to Malach during the Yule of 1914 by Prince Cherkesov, for whom Zoiter worked that year as a watchman, having gone bankrupt, to the very, very last kopek.

"I tinks, Anna Andreyevna, your husband hass already returnt!"

That's what the now-indigent luminoscribe of Annushka's soul told her, upon reflection, during a certain moment of orphan time. And her soul shuddered: Annushka burst into tears of despair, fear, and pity for herself, and for Syomushka, when she fell upon Friedrich Karlovich's chest. And from that moment on, orphan time—to which Zoiter times, with the touch of their radiant edge, had initially, perhaps, but truly imparted some sort of majestic torpor—began flowing differently.

Orphan time began flowing faster and more uneasily, as if it had just been waiting for the luminoscribe Zoiter to unravel the mystery of the stray horse.

The consoling hope that Friedrich Karlovich was wrong hadn't even managed to take shape in Annushka's heart before The Immortal One came within sight of, first, Uncle Alexander, not far from the billiard room, then Uncle Pavel, in the little-known pantry, and, later, Uncle Seraphim, in the Caucasian enfilade of impenetrable rooms.

Before long, Annushka herself caught sight of Malach.

During her search for Friedrich Karlovich—who hadn't put in an appearance in the house's northern region for several weeks, and about whom unpleasant rumors had begun circulating among the spongers, that he'd caught cold and fallen ill—Annushka was in complete solitude and, for the first time in her life, had distanced herself significantly from the lived-in northern expanses, Lavrusha, who'd been accompanying her, having very quickly fallen behind, vociferously cursing his gout. She walked in a southerly direction through a wide corridor with a vaulted ceiling that ran along the Caucasian enfilade and was considered to divide the house into two even parts: the Nogaisk and Tauride. She was walking through the Nogaisk—eastern—half of the house and intended, on Lavrusha's advice, to turn east at the point where the Caucasian enfilade made several completely incomprehensible sharp turns along with the corridor it abutted: there was an absolutely parallel and identical corridor, wide, with a vaulted ceiling, that extended along the Tauride side and shared a wall with the Caucasian enfilade along its entire length, just as its Nogaisk twin did, though it didn't reveal even the slightest curves anywhere.

Annushka sensed an intense dizziness as she approached that place and those spectral Nogaisk sharp turns. Annushka was in no condition to grasp how long that lasted: a minute, an hour, two hours. She only recalled that she never stopped for an instant; she'd continued walking, though now she wasn't walking along a corridor but through a string of small, elongated halls with tall, wide-open doors. At some moment it occurred to her that, just maybe, she'd inadvertently gotten herself into the Caucasian enfilade by turning to the west rather than the east from the corridor where sizeable archways had been coming into view to the right and left, here and there, and in no particular order. The Caucasian enfilade, however, had always been deserted. But these halls were far from deserted. Moreover, they seemed to exist only to perplex or horrify any traveler who fell upon them, though no individual hall contained anything frightening, anything unusual, or even anything Annushka had never seen in other rooms of Malach's house. Everything reminded Annushka of Uncle Pavel's office: the weapons on the walls were, yes, slightly powdery from rust and perhaps even completely falling apart, as was an immense two-handed sword that had disintegrated onto an ottoman but left its contour on a dusty wall, and there were also a raised relief globe, a squat bureau, and tall, carved cabinets. But everything in each next hall was exactly the same as in each previous hall and in the exact same place. The exact same ottoman, exact same globe, exact same disintegrated sword. The halls weren't simply similar; they were absolutely identical, so identical that Annushka only sensed her own fixity ever more firmly and hopelessly as she crossed, faster and faster, from hall to hall. In desperation, she turned in the opposite direction and ran back, but that changed nothing: the feeling she was in the exact same hall each time didn't leave her, so she turned around again, mustered her gumption, and headed in her original direction.

She managed to do that so many times that when noticeable changes appeared in her surroundings she no longer knew which direction she was moving in.

The halls grew much more spacious without losing their elongated form and enfilade arrangement. Now they contained more and more dried-out, splitting furniture, cracked walls, simple and sparse vegetation, and ferocious, lushly swirling cobwebs, which lifted étagères and chairs into the air and led Annushka to understand—and she very quickly understood because she remembered Uncle Pavel's stories—that she was nearing the house's southern confines. A short while later, her eye was met by a hall so vast that it was clear to Annushka she would never reach the burial mound crowned with the kurgan stela that was visible in the distance, let alone the opposite wall. In any case, the archway she'd noticed on the right-hand side of the wall seemed considerably closer. After reaching and walking through that archway, she discovered it had led her into a corridor. And by all indications this was the very same—straight—Tauride corridor that, unlike the Nogaisk, hid nothing insidious within. After finding her bearings and calming herself, she decided to return north, regretting she'd been unable to find Friedrich Karlovich. She'd already taken several steps when a clock's chime suddenly reached her through an archway in the western wall of the corridor: this was impossible in these parts, because, even in the north of the house the steward didn't wind all the clocks, only those that, to his mind, might catch Annushka's eye. Overcoming her fear, she turned into the archway, quickly passed through several smallish rooms, and threw open the partially closed side of a massive double door, finding herself in a gloomy den that was overgrown in spots by wild grass and thorny broom bushes, where the floor clock continued striking, its chime alternating with the sputter of a decrepit mechanism. As she remembered it, she looked, entranced, for a minute or two, at its off-white face, which seemed to be hanging right in the air, like the moon. When the clock's high case and round pendulum, which swung behind cracked glass, began to show, little by little, through the gloom, ruining that wonderful and fleeting sight, Annushka shifted her glance to the side and froze: The Immortal One sat in a sagging armchair a few steps away, bewildering some motionless, waiting lizards with his aimless presence. No! She couldn't be mistaken: she saw his face clearly, saw the frozen, deeply sunken eyes that expressed nothing, neither despondency, nor joy, nor love, nor threat. And before flinging herself out into the Tauride corridor, along which she ran and ran toward the north, having no idea what she was doing, only that she would drop into an insentient sleep in her bedroom, she managed to clearly hear the words The Immortal One uttered, "I'll come to you soon, Anna Andreyevna. And then you can tell me all your dreams . . . And about this head here." Malach lifted from the floor a small, young head in an Austrian military peaked cap. "And about those heads," he added, turning, "that ..."

Annushka, however, did not hear what he added.

EPILOGUE

Four months after that memorable meeting, everything turned out as the Greek had contrived.

Syomushka was liberated from the orphanage at the price of deception, and he became Malach's son, while remaining the son of the inspired Greek. And the storyteller knows nothing further ... Oh, of course, of course, he would like to know many, many things; he would like to know, merciful apostles, what Malach meant by the words he'd uttered in the den in the south of the house, and if Annushka had in fact been there or if her journey was a vision ... Oh, how the storyteller would like to know that! But who could tell him about that now? Who could now transport him from here, from the lost kingdom of Druk Yul, from the cramped Kingdom of Bhutan, from the shores of the rapid-watered Chinchu into the southern Russian steppes and those times that have flowed over them? Would it be you, ruthless Chronos, would it be you, implacable Kala? Or you, the luminoscribes who've simplistically tamed ... time? ... Alas, not time, but only the ghost of a moment, the decayed ghost of a certain chosen moment, preciously sparkling like an indestructible diamond set within an eternity created by God or, as you, my unforgettable Annushka, might say,

in the gold of the Zoiter times.

VLADISLAV OTROSHENKO (born 1959) is a Russian novelist, essayist, and scriptwriter. Born in Novocherkassk, the old capital for the Don Cossacks Army Region, Otroshenko graduated from the Faculty of Journalism of Moscow State University, and is a member of PEN.